KLAWDE

EVIL ALIEN WARLORD CAT

THE
SPACEDOG
COMETH

BY JOHNNY MARCIANO
AND EMILY CHENOWETH

KLAWDE

EVIL ALIEN WARLORD CAT

ILLUSTRATED BY
ROBB MOMMAERTS

PENGUIN WORKSHOP

For the Brooklyn Cat Cafe. Thanks for all
the good work you do, and for Deno—JM

For Esme, cat of my heart—EC

For my elementary school art teacher,
Mrs. Healy. Thanks for all the encouragement,
kindness, and good memories from
the very beginning—RM

PENGUIN WORKSHOP
An Imprint of Penguin Random House LLC, New York

Text copyright © 2019 by John Bemelmans Marciano and Emily Chenoweth.
Illustrations copyright © 2019 by Robb Mommaerts. All rights reserved. Published by
Penguin Workshop, an imprint of Penguin Random House LLC, New York. PENGUIN and
PENGUIN WORKSHOP are trademarks of Penguin Books Ltd, and the W colophon is
a registered trademark of Penguin Random House LLC. Manufactured in China.

Visit us online at www.penguinrandomhouse.com.

Library of Congress Cataloging-in-Publication Data is available upon request.

ISBN 9781524787240   10 9 8 7 6 5 4 3 2 1

PROLOGUE

The Leader of the Pack, Comrade Muffee, called the emergency meeting to order with a howl. When the last echoes faded from the chamber, she turned to the space ranger standing before her.

"Greetings, Comrade Barx," Muffee said. "My fellow Alpha Dogs and I have summoned you here for a matter of the utmost importance. It concerns recently intercepted communications from the planet Earth."

"Earth!" Barx exclaimed. "Do you mean the wonderful planet that is home to the gentle and generous beings known as Humans?"

"The very one," Muffee said. "As you know, thousands of years ago, this distant paradise was spoiled

when our mortal enemies—*cats*—began using Earth as a

maximum security prison."

Her ears instinctively went back, as did those of the

assembled.

"As you also know, we sent our finest peacekeeping

officers to protect the Humans from the feline menace. But when cats stopped exiling their criminals to Earth, our contact with the planet ceased," Muffee said. "What you *don't* know is that our enemies have resumed this despicable practice."

Barx began to growl, but Muffee held up a paw.

"It is even worse than you think. The cat they have sent to Earth is the greatest criminal in the known universe: Wyss-Kuzz the Wicked! Or, as he has become known in his exile, **KLAWDE**."

Comrade Fydo bared her yellow teeth. "No dog will ever forget what he did to us! He must be punished!"

"Now that he is outside the Neutral Zone, we can capture him," shouted Comrade Muzzil. "And make him pay for his crime!"

"Indeed we shall," Muffee said. "Space Ranger Barx, as the bravest and most loyal officer of the entire PUPPS force, I nominate **you** to bring this evildoer to justice."

She turned to the assembled Alpha Dogs. "Do I have the unanimous consent of the Pack?"

"WOOWOOWOOWOOWOO!"

"And do you, Barx, agree to accept this dangerous mission?"

"Yes, Muffee! I do!"

All tails began to wag.

"In that case, comrade, your ship awaits," Muffee said. "There's just one thing you have to do before you go." She coughed awkwardly. "*You* know."

"Uh, I know . . . what?" Barx asked.

The sound of uneasy whimpering echoed throughout the chamber.

"You must . . . *ahem* . . . take off your uniform," she said. "The dogs of Earth live the way the great Doggie Creator in the sky made us. Naked."

Barx gasped. "Even my collar?"

"Goodness, no!" Muffee said. "Earth dogs are still

canines, not mindless beasts!"

"You needn't be ashamed, good comrade!" Fydo said as Barx removed his vest. "It's all a part of the Earth experience. It will help you get in touch with your primal self."

"You may even enjoy such primitive freedoms," Muffee said. "But no matter how sorely you are tempted, do not become bonded to any of the Humans," she warned. "Otherwise, you will be subject to the Master Clause! And if that happens, comrade, your mission may fail."

Barx was down to his collar and license, but still he stood proud. "Don't worry," he said. "I will find this Wyss-Kuzz, and I will make him repay his debt to dogkind!"

The entire Security Pack howled their approval.

CHAPTER 1

"Raj, I need your help!" My dad poked his head into my room, wearing his PLAQUE IS WACK T-shirt. "Do you think I should sign up for the *King of Crowns* lecture, or the *Pearly Gates: Adventures in Tooth Whitening* demonstration?" he asked.

It was a Sunday afternoon, and he and Mom were about to leave for a dental conference—in *Hawaii*. Dad called it "work," but it sounded a lot like vacation to me.

"Wow," I said, yawning. "They both seem really interesting."

"Krish, you need to finish packing," Mom called to Dad. "We can't miss our plane!"

I followed him back to their room. "I can't believe you guys are going to Hawaii without me. And that you're going to miss my birthday!"

"But you have school," Mom said.

Like I'd forgotten! I *wanted* to miss school.

"Besides," Mom went on, "your ajji is very much looking forward to spending this time with you."

Ajji—my grandma. Not my dad's mom, who was funny and bought me all the comics I wanted. But my mom's mom, who could be a little intense. I loved her, but spending two whole weeks with her and my grandpa was going to be exhausting.

"But what about your job?" I asked Mom. "Are you really just going to sit around on a beach instead of doing . . . whatever it is you do?"

"Me, *sit*?" Mom laughed. "I have a weeklong surfing intensive, followed by a week of deep-sea-diver training. Plus I have morning Pilates classes and Japanese lessons at night."

"And *I'm* going to take *Tooth Pics: Advances in Oral Photography* with the coolest dentists in the world!" my dad said. "Then I'm going to do some serious poolside relaxing."

He'd tossed a bunch of clothes into his suitcase, which he was now trying to push shut. Suddenly he yelped and snatched his arm away.

Klawde's paw was poking out from underneath a pair of shorts.

"*Awww*, look at the little stowaway!" Dad said, rubbing his scratched hand. "You want to come to Hawaii, buddy?"

Klawde hissed.

I heard a car pull up, and then the doorbell rang.

"That must be your ajji," Mom said to me. "Go let her in!"

I ran downstairs and opened the door to find my grandma standing on the porch. In one hand, she was holding the handle of the world's biggest rolling suitcase. In the other, she was holding a leash.

Which was attached to a *dog*.

CHAPTER 2

It was a gloriously sunny afternoon, and I was at nap. My sleep was not the death-like slumber of the Humans, but the hyper-aware trance in which all felines plot their schemes. And, oh, what schemes I had! A trio of brilliant inventions, each designed to help me reconquer my home planet.

The only question was which device to launch first. The Zom-Beam, a laser that would turn Humans into my brainwashed soldiers? The Starsucker, a giant battery that harnessed the destructive power of supernovas? Or the Squirr-a-pult, which I think explains itself? All three were under development by my minion, Flooffee-Fyr, in a secret lab far beneath the surface of Lyttyrboks.

In addition to his engineering work, Flooffee kept me informed about the political situation back home.

Happily, my nemesis, General Ffangg, was in prison. But the traitorous calico—the Earth kitten *I myself* had rescued from a life of stupidity and sloth—now reigned with exceptional cruelty from the Most High Throne, and all cats despised her.

Of course I was proud of my protégé. But more importantly, her low popularity gave me the opportunity to overthrow her oppressive regime. And replace it with one of my own!

I rolled over inside my scheming chamber—a device the ogres called a "suitcase." Suddenly, the bald ogre began tossing his garish bodily coverings upon me. The gall!

After slashing him with my claws, I was settling back to nap when the intruder alert rang.

The boy-Human hurried to open the front portal, and that was when I heard the barbaric sound that disturbs the feline soul like no other.

Could it be?

Creeping downstairs, I saw to my horror an ancient, unfamiliar ogre holding the shackles of one of *them*.

The mortal enemy of all felines.

A **DOG**.

My whiskers twitched in revulsion. I had never in my life been this close to a canine, Lyttyrboks being separated from the dog planets by a billion-mile-wide neutral zone. (Which I had once—gloriously!—trespassed. But that is another tale.)

Here on Earth, I had only seen dogs from a distance, as Humans maintained tight control over them. Canines were kept imprisoned inside fortresses or in yards protected by high barricades known as fences. Sometimes they were even contained by force fields connected to shock collars—a most excellent solution!

Because canine discipline seemed to be the one area in which ogres behaved responsibly, I was stunned to witness what the ancient one did next.

She leaned down and unclipped the rope from the canine's collar. The murderous beast was now **free**!

CHAPTER 3

My grandma gave me a giant hug. "It's so good to see you! And look how much you've grown!" Then she turned to the dog. "Wuffles, this is my *mommaga*. That means grandson where I'm from—Karnataka!"

Wuffles came halfway to my knee and had so much white fur it was hard to see his eyes. He was also barking like crazy. "Uh, Ajji," I said, "did you know that we have a cat now?"

"Oh, wonderful!" Ajji said. "We need to find out if Wuffles is good with cats."

But would he be good with *evil alien warlord* cats? And, more importantly, would Klawde be good with a dog?

I turned to see Klawde crouched on the far side of the living room, frozen. His eyes were as big as quarters, and his fur was so puffed out it looked like he'd just been electrocuted.

I had a bad feeling about this.

"Amma!" Mom said, coming into the living room. "You promised you were going to leave all your pets back in New Jersey!"

"I did! Wuffles is a foster dog. I couldn't leave him right after he bonded to me. He'd be traumatized!"

Klawde was now slinking toward Wuffles in a low crouch. I wondered if we were all about to be traumatized.

"Wait—where's Appa?" Mom asked. "I bought two plane tickets."

"Well, Wuffles needed a seat," Ajji said, leaning down to pet the dog, who still hadn't stopped barking. She turned to me. "Raj, I'm sorry your grandpa didn't come, but he couldn't get away from work—unlike some people." She shot a look at my dad.

"But Ajji," Dad said. "This trip *is* work. How else am I going to keep up with the latest trends in designer braces?"

Ajji rolled her eyes, and my dad shrugged. "Let me help you with your giant bag," he said.

"There are two more on the curb."

As Dad went out to fetch the rest of Ajji's stuff, Wuffles suddenly noticed Klawde. He stopped barking and tilted his head to one side.

I looked down at Klawde. Then I looked back at Wuffles. I heard a low, ominous growl, but I couldn't tell which animal it was coming from.

"Is this a good idea?" I asked.

Ajji smiled. "Just let them work things out."

Okay, the growl was definitely coming from Klawde. He took another step toward Wuffles.

Suddenly the dog *exploded*, snarling and barking right in Klawde's face. Klawde turned and ran, racing into the kitchen and leaping on top of the fridge. The dog chased after him, still barking, and Klawde responded, *loudly*.

"My, what an interesting meow he has," Ajji said.

Dad came into the house struggling with the rest of Ajji's luggage. "Are you planning to move in?" he asked nervously.

I heard a honk from outside. It was my parents' cab.

Mom gave me a kiss. "Now be good and listen to your ajji, Raj," she said.

"And happy almost birthday!" Dad said, hugging me.

Mom paused at the door and turned to give me a big smile. "You might want to go check your room for a little special something," she said. "Bye, dear!"

CHAPTER 4

Safe atop the food-cooling apparatus, I stared down at the drooling canine as it repeated its horrible war cry.

"BARKBARKBARKBARK!"

What a strange thing this Earth dog was!

Unlike the Humans, it had the good sense to walk on four legs. It was also less hideous than they were, having the proper anatomical parts: fur, tail, whiskers, and claws. But its snout projected out like a beak, and its whiskers were so stubby and thin they couldn't *possibly* act as intergalactic sensors. Its ears, far from the proud triangular shape of the cat's, flopped over. They were clearly broken.

The ancient texts had much to say about canines. Long ago, cats and dogs lived together on the planet KrittR, in the peaceful epoch known as the Dark Ages. This era ended abruptly in the year 2B, when a dog crossed over into feline territory and peed, in an outrageous attempt to mark it for all dogkind.

The resulting battle between the two species reduced KrittR to a blistering ruin—a place nearly as uninhabitable as Earth. Thereafter, a truce gave cats the vast and magnificent planet of Lyttyrboks to colonize, while canines were given their own solar system, a collection of motley planets known as the Dog Star Cluster.

Although dogs would forever remain cats' most despised enemy, the ancients understood them to be both strong and fearless, and the only opponent truly worthy of felines.

But was this one worthy? Its dark eyes looked up at me with a cold dullness that said *no*.

"BARKBARKBARKBARK!"

Another hint was its lack of vocabulary.

If, over thousands of years, the toxic atmosphere of Earth had so blunted the native brilliance of the feline brain, surely it had affected the canine one as well. But had it also altered the infernal species' other strengths?

I needed to find out.

CHAPTER 5

My present—it was an Okto 4K action camera! With a head mount! It was exactly what I wanted.

I strapped it on my head, and I was filming my parents driving away when Ajji called me into the kitchen to help her unpack her suitcases.

"Um, shouldn't we be doing this in the guest room?"

"I don't need help with my clothes," Ajji said. "I need help with my supplies." She pulled a stack of serving trays—thalis—from the biggest suitcase, and then a pot and skillet. "I had to bring my kadais and tava, and of course my grinder! And where would I find fruits and vegetables such as *these* in this Oregon place?" She pulled out a coconut and some yard beans that were longer than my arm.

"We do have stores here," I said, even though they

probably didn't carry three-foot-long legumes.

Ajji opened the cupboard and held up the garam masala my mom used. "Stores where you buy premixed spices? Ground by a *machine*?" she said, tsk-tsking. "Your ajji likes to do things the old-fashioned way."

I unzipped the other giant suitcase. Everything inside this one was for Wuffles: food, bones, toys, sweaters, about twenty tennis balls, and a box that read: PRINCELY PUP DOGGIE AIR MATTRESS.

"Wow, Wuffles has more stuff than I do," I said.

Meanwhile, he was *still* barking at Klawde up on the fridge.

"Will he ever stop?" I asked.

"Give them time," Ajji said. Then she started throwing all Mom's cooking supplies into boxes.

Mom was not going to be happy about that.

"Can you blow up Wuffles's bed?" she asked. "I didn't have enough room for the electric pump."

I took out the air mattress, breathed in with all the lung power I had, and blew. A corner of the mattress lifted a tiny bit and then settled back down again. I kept blowing, the dog kept barking, and Klawde kept glowering.

Klawde wouldn't attack, would he? I mean, he talked a big game, but he'd had enough of a sense of self-preservation to escape to the top of the fridge.

So why was he wiggling his butt up in the air like he was about to

CHAPTER 6

JUMP!

With all my strength, I made a mighty leap down from my perch, soaring—just barely—beyond the misshapen beast's snapping jaws.

I landed gracefully and then hurtled into the living room. The ferocious fiend took up the chase, following closely at my heels!

I was in immense danger.

Every stride could be my last.

How alive I felt!

I knocked over one of the father-Human's plants as I sprang to the top of the high-backed padded chair. With its stubby legs, the dog couldn't reach me, so instead it ran around in leaping circles, barking madly.

I could not resist a yowl of glee.

"Wuffles, stop tormenting the nice kitty!" called the ancient ogre from the other room.

Nice kitty? She had no idea!

But I could use her ignorance to my advantage.

With a nudge of the paw, I pushed the light-giving device off its perch. It shattered on the floor.

"No, not the lamp!" the boy-ogre shouted.

He had chased us into the room wearing a small plastic device strapped to his head—probably designed to stimulate and strengthen his puny brain—which made him look even more absurd than usual. But I hardly cared about that now. I batted a pillow from the chair, and it hit the canine in the snout.

Then something strange happened. The dog began to attack the pillow! It was as if the beast had utterly forgotten it had a living, breathing enemy with which to do battle.

So this Wuffles *was* a moron.

An admirably strong moron, however. It tore at the fabric with its fangs, pulling out the stuffing and tossing it into the air. In seconds, the dog had massacred it, and yet still the beast growled and snapped at its mangled bits.

"Wuffles, stop!" the boy-ogre cried. "That's Mom's favorite throw pillow!"

Better it than me, ogre.

Now the ancient female came to the edge of the battlefield. "Naughty Wuffles!" she said. "*Sit!*"

Then something truly astonishing happened.

The dog stopped its carnage, let the remains of the pillow fall from its mouth, and sat. It lowered its head and gazed up at the aged one.

I could hardly believe it, but the canine appeared to be displaying one of the Humans' most useless emotions: guilt.

"You mustn't chase the kitty," the ancient one said to the dog. "Now *come!*"

Obediently the dog trotted over to her.

And thus did I discover a remarkable truth: Dogs took *orders* from Humans.

CHAPTER 7

Suddenly I was glad my parents were gone. Because if my mom had seen the living room, she would've called animal control for sure.

The antique lamp was in pieces on the floor. And the throw pillow Mom had hand-embroidered looked like it had taken a trip through the garbage disposal.

At least Wuffles seemed to be ashamed of himself. Klawde, on the other hand, looked proud.

I told Ajji I'd deal with the mess so she could finish unpacking. While I was sweeping up the broken glass, I remembered I was still wearing the Okto 4K. It had been recording the whole time! Maybe there was cool footage of me chasing the dog chasing the cat.

I hurried into my room, where I found Klawde curled up on the bed.

"I know you're the one who knocked over the lamp, Klawde," I said as I connected the camera to my computer. "And Mom's throw pillow! Do you know how hard she worked on that thing?"

Klawde began licking his paw and rubbing it behind his ear, just like he always did when he was particularly pleased with himself. "It was all *Wuffles's* fault. Your grandmother said so. You should listen to your ancients."

"You and I both know it's your fault."

Klawde pushed his ear down. "You can't prove it."

"Oh yes I can," I said, and pressed PLAY.

The picture was bumpy, but it definitely showed Klawde pushing the lamp over and batting the pillow off the chair.

"There's your proof, Klawde!" I said. "Uh, Klawde?"

He'd sprung onto the desk and was staring intently at the screen. His whiskers were twitching in a freaky way I hadn't ever seen before.

"How did you *do* this, Human?" he demanded.

"My cool new camera," I said, holding up the Okto.

Klawde started to purr.

CHAPTER 8

What a magnificent scene! There I was in all my glory, perched high above a furious, pillow-slaughtering canine. In triumph!

The ogre's head camera was laughably primitive, but it was better than the Humans' usual efforts. "How did you acquire this technology?" I demanded.

"I got it for my birthday," the boy-Human said. "Do you celebrate your birthday back on your planet?"

"*Everyone* celebrates my birthday on Lyttyrboks," I said. "Otherwise I have their whiskers plucked out one by one."

But there was no time to explain all the fun and exciting festivities of the Universal Day of the Most Supreme Leader. Because this crude piece of ogre technology changed everything!

I rushed to the bunker to call Flooffee-Fyr and alert him to the change of plans.

"But what about the Squirr-a-pult?" he said. "I really liked that one."

"Those brilliant ideas must be put on hold, minion," I said. "Starting now, we will fight not with weapons, but with *images*!"

"Huh?" Flooffee said.

I explained to him my greatest evil scheme yet. Flooffee would transmit the film of me humiliating the Earth dog to every corner of Lyttyrboks. "All felines will be awed and amazed at my mastery of the canine species. They will fear and worship me!"

"Wait, you met a *dog*?" Flooffee gasped. "And he didn't kill you?"

"He tried," I said. "But I was too cunning. Oh, how I toyed with the beast! And it is only the beginning."

I reminded Flooffee of my long-ago crossing of

the Neutral Zone to visit the Dog Star Cluster. I'd been merely a long-legged cadet, but the little prank I'd played on the canines that day had earned me everlasting fame on my home planet.

But that notoriety would pale in comparison to the reaction I would get when my fellow felines saw **this**!

CHAPTER 9

Klawde seemed to be in an unusually good mood the next morning. He said something about it being a lovely day, which I'd never heard him say before.

I was just pulling on my socks when he asked, "Aren't you forgetting to don your *cool* image-capturing headwear device?"

"I'm just going down to eat," I said. "Do you really think breakfast is going to be that interesting?"

"Oh yes," he said. "*So* interesting."

I shrugged. "All right," I said, and put on the Okto.

It was weird what cats were into.

Downstairs, the kitchen was totally transformed, with copper kadais hanging from the pot rack and glass jars of spices lining the counter. It looked just like Ajji's kitchen back in New Jersey. She lived in Edison, which was just about the most Indian place you could go outside of India itself. The strip malls were filled with Indian supermarkets and restaurants and sari shops, and the local multiplex showed Bollywood movies. It was pretty awesome there.

"Dosa!" Ajji said, placing a silver plate of crispy, potato-filled crepes in front of me. "Your favorite!"

Yum! This was the kind of food my mom hardly ever made, mostly because she was too busy working. And Dad could barely boil water.

"I see you like my breakfast," Ajji said as she watched me devour my second dosa. "So you will love what I packed you for lunch!"

She handed me a heavy blue backpack. I looked inside and saw two stacks of round metal containers.

"Tiffins!" she said.

"What about my regular lunch pack?" I asked. What I really meant was, *What about my regular lunch?*

Ajji tsk-tsked me. "Don't worry! Ajji knows best. You will eat better than anyone else in your school for the next two weeks, I can promise you that."

There was no point in arguing, because Ajji was even more stubborn than Mom.

Plus, I'd just noticed Klawde. He was slinking over to the dog bed, where Wuffles lay sleeping.

"*Klawde!*" I whispered. "*Leave the dog alone!*"

"Did you say something, Raj?" Ajji asked.

"I was—er—talking to Klawde."

"You don't need to be ashamed and whisper!" she said. "I talk to my animals all the time. Which reminds me—I forgot Wuffles's favorite toy upstairs. I can't believe he fell asleep without his snuggybear!"

As soon as she left the room to get it, Klawde said, "Ogre! Take a look at *this*!"

And then he gave the sleeping dog a swipe right across the nose!

CHAPTER 10

It was too easy. First, the gullible young ogre agreed to wear the camera upon his head. (Unlike the dog, I didn't take orders from Humans—I *gave* them.) Then, as the boy-ogre consumed the ancient one's food, I approached the canine.

Its eyes were closed, and it appeared to be napping. Unsurprisingly, this was not the alert nap of the feline, but the drooling unconsciousness of the Humans. Still, I took caution as I approached.

Viewed up close, the canine was even more disturbing than I'd first thought. Its fur, unlike a cat's soft, luxurious coat, was coarse and wavy. Its claws appeared thick and dull—how could it possibly slash an enemy with them? Also, it was now wearing a body covering, of the type the ogres call a "sweater." But why?

The beast *had* fur, unsightly and smelly though it was.

The boy-ogre directed me to leave the dog alone. But I had other plans.

Once the camera was turned in my direction, I was ready for the show to begin.

SLASH!

I struck the dog's nose, claws fully extended. The beast's eyes snapped open as it yelped in shock and pain. When it saw me, it began to growl, a low rumble that sounded like thunder. Then it charged!

Only my superior feline reflexes kept me from the death trap of its snapping jaws. I raced downstairs to my bunker and leaped into the covered sandbox. The dog barked wildly, thinking it had me trapped.

How foolish it was.

When my camera-Human arrived on the scene, I began to kick up sand with my back paws, creating such a flurry that the canine was blinded. Then I sprang back out and landed upon its spine!

The beast yelped and bucked and spun around in circles, desperately trying to throw me off. But I only dug my claws in deeper!

"Klawde, are you out of your MIND?" the boy-ogre cried.

In answer, I spurred Wuffles in the flanks, and back up the stairs we went. I sounded my victory cry as we raced into the living room. But then the ancient ogre sprang out of nowhere and snatched me off the back of the canine! She was quicker than she looked.

The dog whirled around to face me, ready to reengage in battle. Its eyes gleamed murderously as I strained against the iron grip of the she-ogre. Finally, I managed to wriggle out of her clutches and retreat to higher ground. Which just so happened to be atop the ancient Human herself.

"Klawde! Get off of my grandmother!"

CHAPTER 11

It was not the greatest start to a Monday. As if my cat tricking me into wearing my Okto 4K so he could film himself torturing the dog wasn't bad enough, then I had to pull him off of my grandma's *head*. And now I was walking to school with a lunch pack so heavy I could barely lift it. I really hoped no one would notice.

"Hey, what's with the second backpack?" Steve asked the minute he saw me. "Are you trying to get twice as smart?"

"The frightening thing is that you probably believe that's how it works," Cedar said to him. "But why *are* you wearing two backpacks, Raj?"

"I don't want to talk about it," I mumbled.

At lunch, I sat at my usual table. As quietly as possible, I took out the tiffin carriers.

Max leaned over to me. "What the heck is *that*?"

"My lunch," I said, feeling my cheeks get hot. "It's a bunch of different, like, Indian dishes."

I lifted off the lid of metal container after metal container. Ajji had packed me baingan bharta, dal, rice, raita, rasam, mango pickle, coconut chutney, and on and on. In any other place, the smells would be making my mouth water. But not here. Everyone was staring at me, and you *never* want that in middle school.

Max wrinkled his nose. "It smells funny."

"It looks like weird baby food," Brody said.

Then other kids started pointing, too, and whispering over their cafeteria trays of mac and cheese, which was— unlike my baingan bharta—actually disgusting.

I started shoveling the food into my mouth. The faster I ate, the quicker it'd be gone, and then everyone would have to find something else to make fun of.

Scorpion and Newt wandered by on their way to get

seconds of mac and cheese. "P.U.!" Scorpion said, holding his nose. "Where's that *stink* coming from?"

I ignored him, hoping he'd keep walking. But he didn't. He stopped and stood over me.

"I should've known," Scorpion said. "It's from Rat. And he's eating out of little doggie bowls!"

Newt giggled but didn't say anything.

I wasn't hungry anymore, but I kept eating.

No matter how mortified I was, it was still the most delicious food ever.

CHAPTER 12

"The way you rode that dog around the fortress and then sat on top of an ogre—that was SO AWESOME!" Flooffee cried. "No one here can even believe it! They're amazed by how brave and strong you are."

I had to admit: I amazed myself, too.

Yesterday, as soon as the child-ogre left for his pointless school, I had transmitted the video to Flooffee-Fyr to broadcast across Lyttyrboks.

"Instead of calling you Most Hated Wyss-Kuzz, the Tyrant," my lackey said, "they're now calling you Mighty Wyss-Kuzz, Master of Three Species!"

"*Master of Three Species!*" I repeated, purring.

"A faction loyal to you—who knew there was such a thing!—is calling for you to be brought back home," Flooffee said. "The Calico Queen has strung several of these loyalists up by their tails, but it hasn't stopped them. You are the hero of the common cat. *Hard to believe*, right?"

The thought of the miserable Earth kitten gnashing her teeth over my popularity made me purr all the louder.

"When will you send the next video, O Great One?" Flooffee said. "The cats are begging for more."

This was the only sticking point. Today the boy-ogre had returned home in that flaccid form of Human anger they call "being grumpy." Upset that I had tricked him into wearing the image-capture device, he now refused to put it on. Did he not realize he was stalling my glorious return to Lyttyrboks?

In fact, he did not. And he *could* not, because if I told him of my plans, the leaking of the eyes would begin. Then he would beg me not to go, which would both bore and infuriate me.

"So is that it?" Flooffee asked after I told him about the ogre's refusal. "Can't you find another—what do the Humans call it?—'cameraman'?"

I smoothed my whiskers with a paw. "Oh, don't you worry, I have another cameraman in mind," I said, gazing out the bunker's small viewing window. In the citadel across the street, Flabby Tabby lay sleeping. "Or should I say, camera-*cat*!"

Purr.

CHAPTER 13

My phone rang at 1:00 a.m.

"Dad?" I said sleepily. "Why are you calling me in the middle of the night? Is everything okay?"

"Oh, yes, everything's great," he exclaimed. "Is it really that late?"

"Yeah, y'know, *time zones*?"

"Whoops," he said. "Well, as long as I've got you, how are things going?"

I wasn't sure what to say. Should I tell him that Wuffles barked too much, wouldn't fetch, was impossible to take on a walk, *and* had a major farting problem? Or that I suspected Klawde was tormenting him every time my back was turned, and often when I was staring straight at them? Or that Ajji was sending me to school with mango pickles that smelled up the entire cafeteria?

"Everything's fine," I said. "You're coming back next weekend, right?"

"Uh, no. The conference is actually a little *longer* than two weeks, because of the travel time. But Raj, it's so great here! I called because I knew you'd be dying to hear about my super-cool seminars . . ."

From that point on, Dad talked for an hour straight. Since it'd be rude to fall asleep on him, I decided to fix myself a late-night snack. A bowl of dal was spinning around in our new microwave when I started hearing strange noises. I put my end of the phone on mute and walked down to the basement. The sound was coming from the litter box.

"Klawde!" I said. "What are you *doing* in there?"

The sounds stopped. "Uh . . . defecating?" Klawde said.

Since Klawde didn't use the litter box for pooping any more than I did, this was a suspicious answer. I was about to investigate when I realized that my dad was calling my name.

"What? Sorry, Dad—I, uh, might have drifted off for a second there."

"I was just saying that I miss you! How's your grandmother? What about the dog? Are he and Klawde getting along?"

Once again I thought about telling him everything. But what could he do about Ajji's lunches anyway? Or Wuffles's farts?

"Seriously, Dad, everything's totally fine."

Then my dad went back to talking, I went back upstairs to eat my dal, and Klawde went back to doing whatever he was doing in the litter box.

CHAPTER 14

My scheme was working perfectly.

I had attached the camera to the harness that Flabby Tabby's ogre made him wear lately. (She had taken to walking him on a leash like a dog, though I knew from experience he was terrible at this.)

In addition to his filming duties, Flabby also functioned as bait for Wuffles. The idiot dog chased the corpulent Earth cat into every trap I laid out for him.

First, Flabby lured Wuffles into the shower stall, whereupon I locked him inside until he howled in wet despair. Next came the glorious incident of the peanut butter. And yesterday, I shut them *both* inside the dryer and spent a delightful afternoon watching them go around and around.

And around.

And Flabby captured it all on film! He also shot a very unfortunate sequence of himself licking his . . . well, let us not speak of that.

Naturally, the cats of Lyttyrboks ate all this up like fried Zamborxian zettawaffers on a stick! And the most recent episode with the garden hose sparked rioting outside the palace of the Calico Queen, with the entire mob chanting my name!

"Your loyalists—I still can't believe you have them—are preparing a ship to bring you home!" Flooffee had said. "All they need is a *little* more evidence of your mastery of the canine, and they will come get you!"

To this end, I had been working nights in my litter box laboratory, making improvements to the Humans' limited technology. A wire the ogres attached to their ear to make "phone calls" was most useful in communicating with Flooffee, and—even better—I connected the boy-ogre's camera to the Extra-Galactic Feline Image Stream, enabling me to livestream the next event to Lyttyrboks.

I had also been carefully watching the ancient ogre train the canine to perform tricks. (Not that I understood how getting a dog to sit was a trick. Conquering and oppressing millions—now *there* is a trick.)

Finally the moment I had been waiting for arrived.

"I'm going to the store now, little kitty," the ancient ogre said. "You and Wuffles be nice to each other, you hear?"

Nice—yet another Human word we felines do not possess!

As soon as the ancient one was gone, I put Flabby into the camera gear and checked in with my lackey. "Is the crowd ready?" I said into the earpiece.

"*Yes, O Epic Master!*" Flooffee said, his voice barely audible above the sounds of the mob.

"Ohhhh, Wuffles!" I called. "I have a treat for you!"

I waited to hear the click of his claws on the floor. (He could not retract them—dogs are so poorly designed.) Today, however, he did not fall for my ruse. *Hiss!*

I finally found the frightened canine outside under a bush. It was a fine place to hide, except for the fact that his long white tail stuck out from the leaves.

I got Flabby perfectly positioned, and then I spoke in a commanding voice, just as the ancient ogre did. "Wuffles, *come*!"

Unable to resist the command, the dog backed out

of the bush and slunk toward me. He looked stunned and confused.

"Wuffles, *sit!*"

And he did.

"Wuffles, *roll over!*"

And . . . he did!

As he lay there, flat on his back, I put my paw firmly upon his belly, thereby marking him as my inferior.

"Master! O Master!" Flooffee yelled into my ear device. *"The crowd is gasping in amazement! They cry for you to be returned from exile! They wish to crown you emperor for all eternity. The rescue spaceship is being prepared!"*

It was then that I heard a deep and unfamiliar voice, right behind me.

"Wyss-Kuzz of Lyttyrboks!" the voice called. "We meet at last!"

I turned around, and I could not **believe** what I saw.

CHAPTER 15

"If you don't like your grandma's cooking, why don't you just pack your own lunch?" Cedar asked as we walked home from school. "You've got hands. Presumably you can make a sandwich."

It had been day number five of Ajji's tiffin extravaganza—aka the food that was turning me into a social outcast. At least it was Friday and school was over, so I wouldn't have to suffer through lunch for almost three days.

"I don't want to hurt her feelings," I said. "And besides, I *love* Ajji's cooking. It's eating it alone in the hallway that I don't like."

"I love her cooking, too!" Steve said. "That banging bardo thing is crazy good!"

"You mean *baingan bharta*," I corrected him.

Suddenly, Cedar grabbed my arm. "Uh-oh," she said. "I see Cold Bloods ahead."

Scorpion and Newt were leaning on the railing in front of school, eating a bag of chips.

"Yo, Rat! You see this?" Scorpion said, shaking the bag of Krunchitos in front of my face. "This is *real* food."

"Real food? Please," Cedar scoffed. "Those are deep-fried triangles of salt, fat, and GMO corn, which—"

Whatever else Cedar was trying to say got drowned out by the crazy beeping of a car horn. It was my grandmother, driving the family Prius.

"Raj! Raj, it is me—your ajji!" She pulled up right beside us, almost onto the sidewalk. "Are these your nice school friends?"

I looked at Cedar and Steve, and then at Scorpion and Newt. What was I supposed to say: *half* of them are, and the other two are total jerks?

Ajji didn't wait for an answer. "I came to pick you up

so we could get ice cream. T.G.I.F., right? But I can take all of your friends! Come on, children, pile in!"

The thought of me and Scorpion getting ice cream together was horrifying to me, but it was obviously even more horrifying to him, because he grabbed Newt and hurried away.

CHAPTER 16

Standing before me was an abomination greater than anything I'd yet seen on this wretched planet: a *dog who spoke ogre*. It was twice the size of Wuffles, with long yellow fur and large brown eyes.

My tail puffed in loathing. "Who are you?" I demanded. "WHAT are you?"

"I am Space Ranger Barx," the beast proclaimed. "Special agent of the PUPPS Security Pack."

I sank into Defensive Crouch and hissed the Hiss of a Thousand Snakes. PUPPS was a legendary intergalactic canine squadron that patrolled the universe seeking to "do good." Absurd though their mission was, all cats feared them.

Barx stood up, tall and menacing. And then he opened his enormous, fanged mouth.

"So are you loving this planet or *what*?" he said. "I just can't get over it! Earth is so BEAUTIFUL! And all these Humans? They're so good-looking. They smell amazing, too! And check out this fine, strong, naked dog you've befriended. I'm really happy to see that dogs and cats can live together in peace here, just like in the Golden Age. I feel like I died and went to Earth. Oh wait—this *is* Earth!"

I could hardly contain my disgust. "So you came to this wretched planet on *purpose*?"

"Of course! But not because Earth is so fantastic. I came here to bring you to justice—for what you did to Rumpz."

"Rumpz? What is a *Rumpz*?"

"It's a planet. Remember? The one you *blew up*?"

"Ah, 'Rumpz' you call it?" I said. "That's funny. I thought its name was KABLOOIE!"

"Yes, um, *anyway*," Barx went on, "I've got to arrest you. It's a bummer, I know." He made a sad dog face. "You do get to hear all your rights first—that's fun. You have the right to remain silent. You have the right to smell any tree you pass. You have the right to pee on any tree you pass. You have—"

Suddenly a voice spoke inside my ear. "*Master! Are you in danger? All the cats are wondering.*"

Oh no, the cat-cam! Flabby was looking right at us—and beaming everything back to Lyttyrboks! *Hiss!*

"Look," Barx said. "I know our species have been enemies for 20,000 years, but in the spirit of Earth, let's try to get along! I'm taking you back to the Dog Star Cluster—everyone's still pretty upset about you blasting Rumpz to bits—but it doesn't have to be ALL sentencing and punishment. Our solar system is beautiful this time of year. Lots of things to see, really good smells . . . it'll be great!"

"Look, *canine*—"

"Oh, you can call me comrade."

"I will call you whatever I like!" I said, assuming my most majestic voice and facing the camera. "But realize this: You cannot come here and give *me* orders. **I** am the one who gives orders to **dogs**!"

Barx's tail stopped wagging.

"Are you saying that you're not coming with me?"

I scoffed at him.

"Why not?" Barx looked confused. "I asked you so politely."

"Do you not realize who you are dealing with? I am Wyss-Kuzz the Magnificent, Master of Three Species, the greatest feline warlord the universe has ever known! All dogs are my servants. Now *SIT*!"

Barx immediately sank to his haunches. Then he leaped up with a horrified look on his face. "Hey, that's not fair!"

"'Not fair'? Ha! Only the *weak* and the *defeated* believe in fairness."

"Now that isn't very nice," Barx said.

"Do you know what is truly not nice?" I asked, turning so the camera could capture my best angle. "The smell of your fur. Did a Gallassian polefish spray you, or is that your *natural* odor?"

Barx blinked in confusion. "Now it's just starting to sound like you're insulting me."

"That's because I *am*, you slobbering moron."

"But I'm here to take you back—"

"And I'm **not** going with you!" I roared. "So why don't you tuck that pretty golden tail of yours between your shaggy legs and go back to one of the mutt planets I *didn't* blow up!"

Barx bared his teeth. Then he growled. He looked like he was going to say something. But instead, he lunged.

And bit my **tail**!

CHAPTER 17

As we all drove home from Wendy's Waffle Bowl, I couldn't tell if I felt bad because I'd eaten a triple scoop of mint cookies-and-cream in a chocolate-dipped cone with rainbow sprinkles, or because Ajji was suddenly talking about throwing a dinner party.

For the entire sixth grade.

I couldn't think of a more terrible idea, and it was all Steve's fault. He'd told Ajji how much he liked her roti and samosas, which got her started on the topic of all the cooking she'd been doing for me. *Surely*, she said, I had the most beautiful, healthful, delicious lunches in the whole cafeteria. *Surely* every kid was jealous of me.

And I didn't mean to say it, but it just came out. "Why can't you just pack me cheese sandwiches like Dad does?"

Ajji's face went dark, and I felt horrible. She was

silent until we dropped off Cedar and Steve.

Then she turned to me and said, "Raj, we will show them all."

"Huh?" I said.

"I will make a feast, and you will help me. All the children will come and taste this food, and they will love it."

"Ajji, kids my age like hot dogs and hamburgers. *Lunchables*. Do you even know what those are?"

"I can tell by the name that I do not *want* to know," Ajji said.

"But—"

"It will be so fun to spend time with all your friends," she said, cutting me off. "And that nice young man—the skinny one who ran away—make sure he comes, too. He looks like he could use a good meal."

"His name is Scorpion. And he's really *not* a 'nice young man.'"

"Now when should we do it . . . ," Ajji said, tapping the steering wheel and thinking. "Oh, I know! Your birthday!"

I groaned and sank into my seat. How much worse could it get? At least we got home before she decided to hire a clown to make balloon animals.

As we waited for the garage door to come up, we both heard it: the most bloodcurdling shriek in the history of time. And it was coming from our backyard.

"Wuffles?" Ajji said, starting to run.

"KLAWDE!" I yelled, and ran faster.

CHAPTER 18

"YEEEEEEEEEOW!"

The pain—it was like my tail had been blasted by a Zzaxxannian laser torpedo! Fortunately, my cry of agony so surprised Barx that he loosened his grip. I broke free and fled, with Barx a mere whisker's length behind.

Flabby, terrified, raced off in the other direction, taking the camera with him. Thank the eighty-seven moons! I couldn't have the cats back home see what was happening. Namely, that I was running away from a dog.

"STAY!" I yelled over my shoulder. But having tasted blood, Barx was immune to my commands. And now the beast was gaining on me!

Up ahead was the tallest tree in the yard. I raced for it, Barx's jaws snapping right behind me.

BARK BARK BARK BARK
BARK BARK **BARK BARK BARK**
BARK BARK BARK **BARK BARK
BARK** BARK BARK BARK***!***

I reached the base of the tree, sprang up, and caught claws to trunk. In another moment, I was perched on a high branch.

The dog tried to leap after me, but his clumsy paws could not grip the bark.

"What's the matter, *comrade*?" I said. "Oh, that's right. Dogs can't climb trees!"

Overcome with fury and frustration, he answered with a snarl.

"Not so polite now, are you?" I called down.

"WOOF! WOOF! ***WOOFWOOFWOOF!"***

"Master! Master! Are you alive??" I heard faintly.

I adjusted the earbud. "Yes, lackey!" I said. "Alive and well!"

"Oh thank goodness! When that dog got you by the tail and the visual went out, all the cats back here thought you'd been eaten for sure!"

"Ha! It takes more than one alien ranger dog to stop Wyss-Kuzz, Master of Three Species!"

"So you escaped him?"

"Escaped him, why . . . I . . . I . . . *defeated* him. **Yes!**" I said in my most triumphant voice. "The yellow beast is humbled here before me, groveling miserably just like the other one. *Ha! I have no use for you, vile dog! Taste the slash of my claw.* He is now bleeding. It is really quite . . . quite . . . bloody. Yes."

"So, uh, why is he still barking?"

"Oh, those are just his . . . his moans of agony."

"Good news, everybody!" I heard Flooffee say as he proceeded to regale the crowd with the tale of my incomparable feat.

And then the Humans arrived.

CHAPTER 19

Whatever the horrible sound had been, it was followed by an insane burst of angry barks and shrieking yowls.

As soon as I got into the backyard, I stopped in my tracks. A dog I'd never seen before was jumping up and down on his hind legs, like he was trying to climb our oak tree, and madly barking at something in the branches above.

That something was Klawde.

"Hey!" I shouted. "Get away from my cat!"

To my surprise, the dog stopped barking, turned around, and plopped right down on his butt. Then he offered a paw in my direction, almost like he wanted me to shake it.

"Who are *you*, doggie?" I said. "Where did you come from?"

"Be careful," Ajji warned as I walked toward him. "Always approach a dog you don't know slowly."

The dog's tail began to wag and his tongue flopped out of his mouth. He sure *looked* friendly.

"Offer the back of your hand," Ajji called. "Let him smell it."

I did what she said, and the dog carefully sniffed me. Then he licked my fingers and rolled over on his back so I could rub his belly.

"Wow, you're so nice," I said as I scratched him. "What a good boy!"

I heard a hacking sound coming from up in the tree.

"Do you think he's a stray?" I asked Ajji.

"No, he is too well-behaved. And look at that gorgeous coat! He is surely a golden retriever."

I reached into the thick fur under the dog's neck and found a collar with a metal tag. "He has a license," I said. "But the writing on it is weird—it doesn't even look like letters."

Ajji came over and squinted at the symbols. "That's very strange," she said. "Could it be a different language?" She put her hands on her hips and addressed the dog. "We can't contact your owners, Mr. Doggie, if we can't read their phone number. What are we going to do with you?"

"We don't have to take him to the pound, do we?" I asked. "You said they put dogs to sleep there."

The sound coming from the tree was now a purr.

CHAPTER 20

I was most disappointed. The ogres did not take Barx to the place where they "put dogs to sleep." Instead, the boy-Human attached a rope to his collar and led Barx into the dwelling.

What was wrong with these ogres? They were going to allow *another* dog into my fortress? This was just one more reason I had to return to Lyttyrboks as soon as felinely possible.

Still seething, I came inside to eat my dinner— which, I must say, was divine. The ancient ogre had prepared fried white cubes of delectable goodness called paneer. When my dish was empty, I bestowed upon her the rare honor of the Tail Twirl.

I then descended to the bunker to contact Flooffee. Before I could, however, the boy-ogre came down the stairs, with Barx right behind him. The wretched canine was pretending to be an innocent Earth pet, panting with his tongue out like some drooling dimwit. Not that it was much of a stretch.

"What's the story with this dog, Klawde?" the boy-Human asked. "Where did you find him?"

I told him that the dog found *me*, but he remained suspicious. This was ironic, as for once I was actually innocent. Not innocent of exploding a planet, obviously, but of summoning this moronic mutt to my yard.

"Then how do you explain his tag?" the boy-Human asked. "It looks like alien writing. Like *your* writing."

The thought that the ignorant scrawl of the dog planets could be mistaken for the intricate script of Lyttyrboks sickened me. I stayed silent, however, as I did not want the boy-ogre to know that Barx was a space ranger seeking to arrest me.

Barx, too, obviously felt the need to keep his

identity a secret. Or maybe he just enjoyed acting like a dumb Earth dog.

"Aww, look at the way he's licking me, Klawde! Isn't it *soooo* cute?"

It was not.

The young Human turned to go upstairs. "I don't know what you're up to, Klawde," he said. "But be nice to the doggie!"

"*Nice*—remind me what that means again?"

The moment the two of them were gone, I called Flooffee, who answered eagerly. "Hey, lord and master! The cats here sure are impressed by how you defeated that doggie ranger. The bards are yowling your praises, and the Calico Queen has been forced to allow your return. I hear they're even going to give you a parade. I just love a parade!"

"But what about the ship to bring me home?" I asked.

"That's the best news of all!" Flooffee said. "I'm IN

it. The bummer is that it's one of our slower models, so we won't get there until tomorrow. I'd say around noon, ogre time."

This was it! It was *really* happening. My rescue was imminent! I was to return home—in **triumph**! Oh, purr of all purrs!!

The only thing that could possibly ruin my plans

was Barx. I needed to make sure he stayed out of my fur long enough for me to escape this awful wasteland.

I found the beast in the kitchen. The boy-ogre had made a bed there for him—a nest of blankets, a pillow, and one of Wuffles's "special" stuffed bears—and Barx was sound asleep in it. Snoring, just like the bald ogre. I reached out and poked him in the flank. No response. I looked around to make sure we were truly alone.

And then I bit him on the leg.

"That's for my tail, canine," I said. I steeled my nerves and prepared for a counterattack.

But Barx merely yawned. "Look," he said, "I know I have to catch you and make you face justice and all, but can we do that in the morning? I'm exhausted from chasing you up that tree, and if I don't get my twenty hours of sleep a day, I'm not really good for much."

He yawned again and gave a long stretch of his front legs.

"Besides," he added, "I can't capture you when Humans are in the house. I'm not allowed to let them know who I really am. Leader of the Pack's orders, and I'm not *fe-lyin'* to you. Get it? Like feline, but it's *fe-lying*? Funny, right?"

And thus another ancient observation was proved correct: Dogs have the worst sense of humor in the universe. But this new information from Barx cheered me. By the time the ogres finished their lunch, I'd be long gone in the rescue pod!

As I turned tail to leave, Barx bid me good night. "And good luck with all your plans," he added, rolling over onto his back.

With all my plans? Did the dog suspect something? Did he *know* something?

Impossible. He was strong, yes, but so obviously dull-witted that I had nothing to fear.

CHAPTER 21

When I came downstairs the next morning, the new dog was waiting for me in the kitchen, wagging his tail and practically begging me to come play with him. I'd never had anyone look that happy to see me before, not even my own parents. And definitely not Klawde.

"*Aww*, who's a good boy!" I said, rubbing his ears. "Should we go outside?"

I grabbed one of the tennis balls Ajji had brought for Wuffles, and the dog and I went into the yard.

"Do you know how to fetch?" I asked him. "Do you, boy?"

He actually seemed to be thinking about the question.

I threw the ball and said, "Go get it!"

He hesitated, glancing back and forth between me and the ball. For a moment, he locked eyes with me, cocking his head to one side. Then he spun around and went racing after the ball. He picked it up, trotted right back to me, and dropped it at my feet.

"Let's do it again!"

Wag, wag, wag.

It was kind of weird to talk to an animal and have it not talk back. Weird, but not necessarily bad. I didn't miss being called an imbecile.

I threw the ball until my arm got sore. And then I threw with the other arm. This dog couldn't get enough!

Finally, after we'd played fetch for at least an hour, the dog flopped at my feet, panting. I sat down next to him and petted his amazing golden fur. "I wish you could stay with us for a while," I said. I looked again at the tag on his collar. What in the world did it *say*? "I'm going to call you Roscoe until we find your real owners. Okay?"

The dog's tail flopped against the ground. I think he approved.

"Raj!" Ajji called from the kitchen. "Breakfast time."

When I went inside, Ajji handed me a plate of dosa.

"You know, your cat is very peculiar," she said. "This morning I saw him staring at the newspaper, like he was pretending to read it."

"Yeah, pretending," I said. "That's funny."

"He likes paneer, so he is obviously smart. Still, he'll never be able to do cute tricks like a dog," she said, and looked over her shoulder. "Isn't that right, little Wuffles?"

Wuffles barked, then farted.

CHAPTER 22

I waited high in the tree for my escape pod to arrive. Nothing, not even watching the boy-ogre and Barx cavort through the yard in a revolting display of joy and mutual affection, could dampen my mood.

What would be my first act upon being reinstated as Supreme Leader? Should I raise massive taxes to build myself a new palace? Slash the furcare budget? Release Ffangg from prison and then lock him back up again? Return the calico to Earth?

No, that would be *too* cruel. I would shave all her fur and make her wear clothing instead.

The boy-Human exited the yard, and Barx came over to my tree.

This would be tedious.

"Hey, how come you're up in the branches again,

Klawde? I hope you're not scared of me," he said. "Like I told you, I won't catch you while the Humans are around."

My ears flattened. "You surprised me once, canine, and all you got was my tail. You could stay for ten thousand more sunrises and you wouldn't catch any more of me than that!"

"We'll have to see about that, I guess."

"You'll never get the chance," I muttered.

Just then, my earpiece exploded. *"Lord and master!"* Flooffee said, his voice now as clear as if he were standing next to me. *"We just passed through the Andromeda galaxy! We're almost there!"*

I could hardly contain my excitement. I was mere moments from my deliverance!

"What's that noise?" Barx said, his ears pricking up. "And what's that in your ear?"

"Oh, it's nothing," I said. "Why don't you run along

and play your chase-the-flying-round-object game with the ogre some more?"

Barx wagged his tail. "That Human, you sure lucked out with him. What an extraordinary animal he is!"

"*My* Human?" I said. "The one they call *Raj*—that's who we're talking about?"

Granted, he was less offensive than the other ogres, and he had proved himself useful on several occasions. But **extraordinary**? I could hardly see how *that* word would apply.

"The way he loves to play! He throws the ball so straight and so far. I tell you, I haven't had this much fun since I was a puppy in a litter of fourteen!" Barx sighed. "Oh, Humans are so wonderful. I sure will miss them after I arrest you and go home."

Suddenly, in my ear: "*We are here, lord and master! We are about to enter the Milky Way. Oh wonderful day! We will get to you in moments!*"

"Well, Barx," I said, "you and the Human can have each other. For if you plan on staying on Earth until you arrest me, you shall stay forever. For I, Wyss-Kuzz the Magnificent, Master of Three Sp—"

"Lord and master!"

"Be quiet, fool!" I yelled into the microphone. "I am delivering my evil genius speech."

"But we, uh—well, we have a problem," Flooffee said. *"We're stuck."*

"Stuck? What do you mean *stuck*?"

"There's some kind of force field surrounding the Milky Way. It's preventing us from getting in. It's like nothing I've ever seen before!"

"Well, blast through it, fool!"

"I'll try, master, but it's some seriously advanced technology. I don't know who could've done this."

Who? Who indeed! Which of my archenemies? The Calico Queen? General Ffangg? Tarkkwwyn the Tormentor?

"So, what's going on up there, 'O lord and master'?"

I looked down at Barx, who was grinning his grotesque doggie grin at me.

No—I couldn't believe it.

"It was **you**!" I cried. "You slobbering, stinking pile of fur! How did you do this? How did you know?"

"We 'dimwit' dogs have been intercepting your communications with Lyttyrboks for weeks," he said, wagging his tail. "How do you think we even knew you were *on* Earth?"

I was in such a rage that my immense vocabulary failed me! I hissed and spat.

"Anyway, I *am* sorry to mess up your travel plans, Klawde," the miserable mutt said. "I know how much you want to go home. But you're going to the Dog Star Cluster instead."

With that, the canine turned and left. I could only muster a single word, spoken with all the fury that had ever fueled my warrior soul:

CHAPTER 23

On Sunday, Cedar and Steve came over to meet Roscoe, who wagged his tail so much when he saw us that Steve got worried it was going to fall off. And when I asked Roscoe if he wanted to play fetch, it was like he nodded *yes* at me!

My arm was so sore from yesterday that my first throw sailed way off. But Roscoe raced under it, leaped into the air, spun all the way around in a twisting somersault, and landed with the ball in his teeth.

"Wow!" Steve said. "Did you train him to do that?"

"No, he just does that on his own! Because he's *awesome*," I said, scratching him behind the ears.

Cedar and Steve were amazed by all the tricks Roscoe could do. He could shake, walk on his hind legs, speak, and give high fives. Cedar was trying to teach him how to dance when Ajji poked her head out the door.

"Raj," she said, "it's time to come inside. We have to make the FOUND DOG posters."

My heart sank. It was super selfish, but I never wanted to find Roscoe's owners.

I think Cedar could tell, because as she petted him goodbye, she said, "It'd be great if you could keep him."

And why *couldn't* I? Plenty of people had a cat and a dog. Steve had two dogs and a hamster, and Cedar's cousins had a whole farm full of goats and sheep!

When I asked Ajji about it, she looked at me like I'd gone nuts. "First of all," she said, "Roscoe's owner is *somewhere*. And second of all, your mother wouldn't allow it. Not in ten lakh years!"

Since ten lakh means a million, this was basically her way of saying never. And as much as I hated to admit it, she was right.

I took a picture of Roscoe to put on the poster. He

licked my hand, like he was trying to comfort me.

"I swear, it's like he knows exactly what I'm feeling," I said to Ajji.

"Dogs are very intuitive," she said. "Isn't that right, Wuffles? No, boy, put your ajji's shoe back."

When I went upstairs to make the poster, Klawde was lying on my bed. As I began to type out the description of Roscoe, he came over to look.

FOUND DOG

Friendly, intelligent, well-trained golden retriever. Gentle but strong, he is able to answer to all commands.

"Are you serious?" Klawde said, reading over my shoulder. "Try: *Caught Trespassing: Pompous, insufferable, insipid mutt. Underhanded and smug, he answers to the name of* Moron."

"Klawde," I said. "If I didn't know you better, I'd say you were jealous of him."

He hissed at me.

"Ogre, you have no idea how he plagues me! The cretinous cur thwarts me at every turn! He usurps my place, upsets my best-laid—"

"What are you so grumpy about?" I interrupted him. "You don't even *like* to play fetch."

He hissed again and left.

Cats. I would never understand them.

CHAPTER 24

After dinner, the young ogre shackled Barx with the leash and led him away on a forced march. I took this opportunity to call Flooffee via a secure line on the intergalactic communicator.

When I asked my minion if he had made it through the force field yet, he informed me that he had abandoned his position and returned to Lyttyrbuks.

"You cowardly scoundrel!" I cried. "You must come back at once and try again!"

"But O Supremest One, there was nearly a mutiny on the ship," Flooffee said. "Until I break the force field's encryption code, there's no way I'll get the loyalists to come back with me." He added, muttering, "Not that they're even that loyal anymore . . ."

"What did you say? Speak up, dolt!"

"Oh! Uh, well, with you stuck on Earth, your poll numbers are way down. The Calico Queen is claiming that you're afraid to come back, and Ffangg—well, he's out of prison now and working as the queen's spokescat. He's really quite charming, in his own—"

"Silence! I order you to fix this! To break the encryption! To resend the ship—"

"Oh, hey, what's that, your highestness? *KSH-KSH!* So much static! You're breaking up, Invincible Master! *KSH-KSH!*"

"Stop doing that! I never fall for it!"

Flooffee sighed. "Look, I'm sure I can figure out this force field thing. After all, you say the canines aren't that smart, so how hard can it be to hack their system? In the meantime, you have to sit tight."

He wanted me to *sit tight*? Ha! Idleness was not an option for a warlord. What I needed was to take matters into my own paws.

CHAPTER 25

I'd just come into the kitchen after an early morning walk with Roscoe when Ajji handed me a bowl of pongal and a notebook. "Here," she said. "Breakfast, and the menu for the feast!"

With all the Roscoe excitement, I was really hoping she'd forgotten about the birthday party.

"Oh no, I did not forget!" Ajji said, as if reading my mind. "I have decided on most of the dishes, but I need you to look the list over. This is *your* party after all!"

Actually, it wasn't mine. It was hers. But I didn't think I could make her understand that.

Luckily my phone rang. It was Mom.

"How's Hawaii?" I asked. "Do you know how to surf yet?"

She was telling me about how she'd just gotten

"locked inside her first tube"—whatever *that* meant—when Wuffles started barking for his breakfast. And then Roscoe joined in, even louder.

"Raj," she said sharply. "Are there *two* dogs in my house now?"

"Well . . . ," I began.

"What is my mother doing?" she practically yelled into the phone. "Opening a kennel?"

Ajji went red.

"Oh, Mom. It's not like that at all!" I said quickly. "Roscoe just showed up in our yard the other day, and we're working really hard to find his owners. He's a great dog, Mom. You'd love him."

"Interesting," she said. There was a long pause, and I heard her take a sip of something. "Well, I'm glad you're trying to help him get home. Just make sure it happens sooner rather than later."

"Don't worry, Mom. We'll take care of it."

"How is everything else going? Do you like your new camera?"

I couldn't admit that I hadn't used it since Klawde tricked me, and that I didn't even know where it was at the moment. "It's great, Mom. The best birthday present ever."

After I hung up, Ajji said, "Good job with your mother," and patted me on the shoulder. "Now help me with the menu."

Sighing, I scanned down the list of dishes. If we served this stuff to the kids from school, they'd make fun of me forever. I couldn't even pronounce half the dishes on the list. *Allugedda?* What was that?

Also, practically everything was a vegetable. Which made sense, us being vegetarians and all, but I bet Brody hadn't eaten anything green in years.

"Could we, um, have some tortilla chips?" I asked. "Maybe some salsa?"

Ajji clucked her tongue and handed me a stack of

envelopes. "Here," she said. "All twelve invitations. You can hand them out at school today."

My stomach felt queasy. It was great that I'd talked her down from inviting the whole class, but *written* invitations? What decade did she think this was?

"And make sure you tell them: *Come hungry.*"

CHAPTER 26

Finally! The fortress was ogre-free, and I could initiate my *new* plan: to make Barx so miserable that he would abandon his mission and slink home in defeat. And in order to do so, he would have to lower that infuriating force field.

Owing to Barx's size, it was unwise to engage him in a full-frontal attack. But though the canine had brute strength on his side, I possessed the vastly superior attributes of stealth and cunning.

Which was why, late last night—when cats roam their territory, and dogs lie in a snoring stupor upon their beds—I had scouted the fortress and chosen the site of my ambush.

To an Earth dog, there is no more delectable liquid than the water found inside the white porcelain fountain in the bathroom. I had yet to sample it myself, for obvious reasons. I pooped in it. (And far worse, so did the ogres.)

But the imbecilic Wuffles had somehow informed Barx of its deliciousness, and so I curled up behind the toilet bowl to hide. I waited many naptimes. My claws itched to slash the canine's huge, hideous snout!

And finally I heard it—the click of toenails along the floor. A moment later, the beasts came into the room.

"Please, Wuffles," Barx said. "After you."

I heard the sound of Wuffles *slurp-slurp-slurp*ing the toilet water while Barx panted eagerly, waiting his turn.

He wouldn't get it.

I sprang from my hiding place, claws fully extended! My left paw slashed Barx's nose, my right his ear. Barx stumbled backward in shock.

"What the *heck*?" he said.

I used Wuffles's back as a launching pad and hurled myself into the hallway, hitting the ground full stride and racing away.

Barking wildly, the dogs took up the chase.

How clumsy these mutts were, scrabbling madly along the floor! I leaped to the mantel and flung down a stack of books that the father-ogre kept there. They hit Barx on the shoulder, and he yelped in anger. After that, I launched a vase at Wuffles. By some miracle, he dodged it, and roses scattered across the rug.

I crouched down. My hips waggled as I prepared for liftoff.

Soon I was sailing over their dumbfounded faces. I continued the chase down to the bunker, where I had prepared my final strike.

Perched atop the father-ogre's recliner, I waited as they made their clumsy, thundering descent of the stairs. As they spotted me and began to close in, I reached down and pressed the button on the armrest.

The bottom half of the recliner shot out, flinging

Wuffles into the air. He did a full somersault before

landing on his back in the potted fern. It was brilliant!

Barx snarled. He was about to lunge at me, but then

he stopped and sat down.

Whatever for?

Did he want to call a truce?

My strategy was working! Already Barx was giving up. But I wasn't finished with him yet. I jumped down and clawed him on his nose.

"**Bad cat!**" said a voice.

I looked up and saw the ancient ogre, glaring at me from the staircase.

"No paneer for you tonight, kitty!"

Barx slunk over to her, whimpering and whining. He looked so wounded and pathetic that if I were capable of pity, I might have felt it.

"Poor doggie," the ogre said. "It's a good thing I came home, or who knows what this naughty kitty might have done to you! Don't worry. I'll make you something special for dinner tonight."

The minute the ancient one left, Barx got up and began wagging his tail.

"You fraud!" I hissed. "You sniveling charlatan!"

"Actually, you really did hurt my nose," Barx said, giving me his stupid sad dog look. "*And* my feelings."

"BAH!"

This outrage would not go unpunished.

CHAPTER 27

After school, I started putting up the FOUND DOG posters around the neighborhood. I felt sick about it. For one thing, I didn't want Roscoe to go. For another, I was worried. What if Roscoe's owners weren't good people? They'd obviously done a terrible job of keeping him from getting loose. And did they play with him as much as I did? Did they feed him paneer? (That was one thing Klawde and Roscoe had in common: They both loved paneer.)

I was taping a poster to a telephone pole when my neighbor Lindy called out to me.

"Hey, Raj! Look at Chad walk on a leash!"

I looked. *Walk* was an overstatement. It was more like he was being slowly dragged across the street. His furry folds were spilling out through the straps of his harness. I could see why Klawde called him Flabby Tabby.

"Don't you think that thing's a little tight?"

Lindy ignored my question. "Not many cats can be trained to walk on leashes, but Chad can! Isn't he the smartest cat?"

"*Mrowr?*" Chad said.

"Yeah," I said. "The smartest."

"My parents say they'll get me a dog if I promise to take it out for walks, so I'm showing them how good I'd be," Lindy said. "You're so lucky that you have *two* dogs now."

"Well, we're looking for the real owners of Roscoe," I said, nodding at the poster I'd just taped up.

"But Wuffles—he's the cute one! Especially his name!"

"You like *Wuffles?*" I asked, surprised. "Well, you can have him. Ajji is only fostering him. He's up for adoption."

"Really?" Lindy said, her eyes going wide. "That's awesome! I'll talk to her at dinner!"

"What dinner?"

"Your birthday party, silly!" she said. "Both of us are going!"

"Both of who?"

"Me and Chad! Your grandma saw me walking him the other day and invited us! It's going to be so great!"

It was all I could do not to bury my face in my hands.

CHAPTER 28

Barx!

He had bitten my tail, invaded my fortress, intercepted my communications, blocked my escape, and even gotten my paneer rations taken away.

Clearly, I had underestimated the enemy. I should not have doubted the wisdom of the ancients—dogs are indeed the only foe worthy of the cat.

But the battle was far from over. I was presently crouched deep inside the tall mesh basket the Humans used to store their soiled bodily coverings. The stench was dreadful, but it was a most comfortable hiding spot.

This "hamper" was kept in the room in which I had put Wuffles and Flabby through those amusing spins in the dryer. Rest assured, *they* had never returned to this place. Barx, however, came here once a day when the ogres were gone, and he always locked himself inside. Now I would find out what he was up to.

I was in the midst of my seventh nap when I heard Barx approaching. Peering out through a foul-smelling Human sweater, I watched as he closed the door, pushed the lock button with his nose, and quickly swiped at his collar with a hind paw.

What was he doing?

The shiny metal medallion hanging beneath his chin began to glow red. Of course! I should have known the canine's collar was not like the primitive strangulation devices employed by the Humans.

My fur stood on end as a hologram of a spacedog flickered into view. This one was small, with brown-and-white fur and extremely long, drooping ears. Like a Human, it wore an ugly yet intricate body covering.

"Greetings, Comrade Muffee!" Barx said. "Comrade Barx, reporting in."

"Yes, I can see that," the holo-dog said curtly. "So tell me, is the criminal cat in your custody yet?"

"Well, not *yet*," Barx said. "But my intelligence-gathering operation is going really well!" Barx's tail began to wag slightly.

The holo-dog frowned. "Might I remind you that this is *not* your mission?"

Barx's tail stilled itself. "But I'm the first canine to make contact with one of our long-lost cousins in *thousands* of years!"

"The Earth dog known as Wuffles, you mean?" the holo-dog asked. "Has this relationship begun to yield useful information?"

"Well, I still can't understand anything he's saying. But I really like him! Oh, and he *did* show me this amazing water fountain." Barx began wagging his tail again.

"The Humans remain ignorant of your true identity, I trust?"

"Yes, of course. Have I mentioned how wonderful they are?" Barx said. "I love everything about them."

I had to choke back several hairballs as the fool went on to praise every last thing the ogres did.

"Earth does indeed sound like the paradise our foremothers told us it would be," said the hologram. "I understand your desire to linger. But *when* will you bring the feline to justice?"

"Soon! I promise, Comrade Muffee. I only wish I didn't have to leave Klawde's Human. I really do love that kid."

The hologram flickered. "The feline has a *Human*?"

"Yes, a most excellent boy named Raj."

"This complicates matters," the hologram said.

"What do you mean?" Barx asked.

"The Master Clause does not apply *only* to dogs," Muffee said. "This ancient rule states that if any four-legged being accepts the hospitality of a Human for a prolonged period—or engages in significant inter-species playtime—the Human becomes his or her *master*. So is this Raj indeed Wyss-Kuzz's master?"

"Um, I guess so," Barx said.

How ridiculous! Raj, my master? *I* was the master. Any idiot could see that.

The holo-dog frowned. "If indeed the cat belongs to this Raj, then you need the boy's permission to take him to the Dog Star Cluster."

This was excellent news! The child-ogre would never betray me. And then I began to purr, for I'd realized an even more delicious consequence of this rule—one which had clearly just occurred to Barx as well. He began to pant nervously.

"Is something wrong, Comrade Barx?" Muffee asked.

"Well, um, I have a confession to make." Barx paused. "I . . ." He paused again. "I have also accepted hospitality from the Human. And . . . I played *fetch* with him."

"Barx! Did I not **warn** you?" Muffee thundered. "This means that you too are subject to the Master Clause! Now YOU must do whatever the Human says!"

Barx's formerly proud tail sank down between his legs. "Don't worry, I can still complete my mission. The feline isn't half as smart as he thinks he is."

Only my need for secrecy kept me from mauling the beast for such a preposterous lie.

"I certainly hope you're right," she said. "All the inhabitants of the Dog Star Cluster are counting on you."

The hologram grew blurry, and Comrade Muffee was gone.

Barx sighed, clicked off his collar, and left the room.

I remained where I was, contemplating the situation. No doubt this Master Clause would prove useful. But the task at hand remained the same: I needed to lower the force field. And surely the mechanism controlling it was *in that collar*.

CHAPTER 29

"Did you hand out all the invitations today?" Ajji asked as she dipped a zucchini pakora in some tamarind sauce.

"Sort of," I mumbled.

Honestly, at first I'd just thrown them into my locker. I didn't want to let *anyone* know about the party. But then I thought about how disappointed Ajji would be when no one came, and how she'd call my parents to say that I didn't have any friends. And that would be all the excuse my mom needed to sign me up for ballroom dancing or some other horrible after-school activity.

"What do you mean, 'sort of'?" Ajji asked.

"I mean yes," I said. "I gave out all of them."

I didn't mention that I hadn't invited Scorpion, or that Ajji was probably the only person in the world who thought he was "a nice young man."

"Excellent! We will have such a good time."

"Uh, yeah," I said, picking at the leftover fried bits of pakora. It was a test recipe for the party, and it was delicious. "Did you get any calls about Roscoe?"

Ajji shook her head.

"Neither did I," I said. "What if we *can* keep him? Mom really didn't want Klawde, either. Maybe she'll change her mind about Roscoe, too. Maybe she'll even love him. I mean, he does so many tricks!"

"Can he do laundry? Mow the lawn?" Ajji asked, raising an eyebrow. "Those are the kinds of tricks that would interest her."

"She can't even get *me* to do those tricks."

"Good point," Ajji said, smiling. "There is no doubt Roscoe is an excellent dog. That cat of yours, however, he is something else . . ."

"What? You don't like him?" I said.

"I love *all* animals!" she said. "It is just that Mr. Klawde is very strange. I have never seen him sit on your lap. He does not like to be petted. And his purr sounds nefarious. Not that a little fuzzball like him knows what *nefarious* means, of course."

"No," I said, popping the last pakora crumbs into my mouth. "Definitely not."

CHAPTER 30

Nighttime. A warrior's favorite hour, when the nefarious enemy lies vulnerable in sleep! I padded downstairs to the kitchen, where the miserable curs lay grunting and whining in their doggie beds.

With noiseless grace I sprang to the counter. Passing over Wuffles's smelly strap of leather, I snatched Barx's collar from its hook. The metal tag jangled, but it did not disturb the comatose snoozing of Barx.

Some space ranger *he* was.

I took the collar down into the bunker to examine it, calling Flooffee for technical assistance.

"Greetings, flunky," I said. "I am giving you the chance to redeem yourself."

"How can I help, O Great One?" Flooffee said.

I held the collar up to the communicator. "I need to

gain access to this canine device."

Flooffee squinted at it. "Oh, that's simple enough," he said. "Just plug the communicator's flix cord into the collar's psylo-port, and calculate $-\beta\pm\mathring{A}\sqrt[3]{\overset{\text{def}}{=}}\omega\times M$ when $M = 49.873514$. Then refractate the result with the Torg algorithm and—"

"Enough, I get it! Do you think I am some idiotic Earth cat?"

"Of course not, Supremest Leader! Forgive me."

From there, it was kitten's play to find the remote control app for the force field.

"Flooffee, get the escape pod ready!" I said as I pressed **FORCE FIELD UNLOCK**. Then a prompt popped up, asking me for the password.

Curse the eighty-seven moons!

I considered the question for a moment. How did this spacedog's mind work? Then I entered:

BONE

Access denied.

FETCH

Access denied.

#TOILETWATER

Access denied.

I_LOVE_HUMANS

Access denied.

At this point something unfortunate happened.

MAXIMUM NUMBER OF ATTEMPTS EXCEEDED.

PROCEED TO LOCKDOWN.

The tag of the collar glowed, and in the next instant, a web of lasers surrounded me. I was trapped!

Curse you, Barx!

CHAPTER 31

I woke up really late on Tuesday morning. Klawde hadn't bitten my toes and yelled "Get up, fool!" like he usually did, but I didn't have time to wonder where he was. I got dressed and ran down to the kitchen. Barx and Wuffles were still sleeping, and Ajji was drinking her tea. She handed me some idli—a kind of spongy rice cake—and I headed for the door.

"Call me at school if anyone comes for Roscoe," I yelled back. "Don't let him go before I say goodbye."

"Of course, dear," Ajji said. "Have a wonderful day!"

In homeroom, our remote teacher, Miss Emmy Jo, flickered onto the smart screen the second the bell rang. "Well, good morning, children!" she said, grinning at us. "I hope y'all are ready for another day of good ol' fashioned book learnin'! I hear there's a pop quiz in math—but don't tell Ms. Rice I told y'all. And I *also* hear that Mr. Student Number Twenty-Seven is having a little birthday party!"

She looked right at me, and I tried to sink lower in my seat.

"I sure am sorry I can't make it, but it just isn't possible for me to get on a big ol' plane and fly a couple thousand miles to eat dinner with y'all." She glanced down at a piece of paper and then back up at me. "You can understand that, can't ya, Rage?"

"It's *Raj*," I said. "But yeah."

What I couldn't understand was how Miss Emmy Jo had even *heard* about my birthday party. But then again, she seemed to know a lot for someone who'd never set foot inside our school.

I wondered if Scorpion and Newt had heard about the party, too, because that was the last thing I needed. As I hurried down the hall to English class, though, I realized I had no reason to worry. Even if they did hear about it, there was no way they'd ever show up.

CHAPTER 32

The Humans had left long before I heard the sound I had been dreading: the *click click click* of Barx's clumsy canine nails.

"Well gosh golly, what have we here?" the mutt asked, inspecting my prison. "Gee, Klawde, I have to thank you

for doing my work for me. That really was too easy."

"This is an outrage!" I spat.

"Nope, it's a *trap*," Barx said.

I could hear the smug pride in his voice. Oh, if I could only get my claws on him!

"Wyss-Kuzz, I hereby arrest you for crimes against dogkind. You know your rights, because I read them to you already. Well, the important ones, anyway. I will now transport you to the High Canine Court, where you will—"

"*SIT!*" I roared.

His tailside dropped to the floor.

"Dang it!" Barx said. "Stop doing that. Now where was I? Oh, right. Prepare yourself for a journey to the Dog Star Cluster. As I said, it's lovely this time of year."

"Ah, Barx," I said with a twitch of my whiskers. "Aren't you forgetting something?"

"Hmmm. I begged at breakfast. I barked at a squirrel. I peed the perimeter of the yard. Nope, I think I got it all covered."

"But what of . . . THE MASTER CLAUSE?"

Barx's tail went down and he pinned his ears back.

"How do *you* know about that?" he said.

"In matters of espionage, the feline will always be your superior!"

"*Grrrr!*" he growled.

Barx looked ready to attack, lasers or no. But after a moment, he calmed himself.

"Klawde, you leave me no choice," he said, thrusting his snout into the air. "I must reveal my true identity to Raj. Then he will give me his permission to take you to the Dog House."

My tail puffed in shock. "But you are under orders not to reveal your identity!"

"Unless there is no other choice," he said. "And you're not leaving me any."

"If you tell the boy-ogre who you are, then I will tell him he has to send *you* home!" I declared. "He is your master now, so you must do whatever he commands!"

"It doesn't matter. I have faith in the Humans, and in Raj most of all." Barx pressed a button on his collar. "You're free to go—for now. I know Raj will side with me, once I appeal to his sense of right and wrong."

I groomed my whiskers, disguising my growing alarm. *Appeal to his sense of right and wrong?* How could I combat something I could not even begin to understand?

CHAPTER 33

Ajji picked me up after school because it had started to rain really hard. I was happy for the ride until she told me that we weren't going home. Instead we went to Vij's, an Indian grocery forty-five minutes away in St. Helena.

She browsed every aisle twice, made five new friends, and bought enough groceries to fill the entire back seat of the Prius. By the time we got back to the house, it was nearly dark.

I walked inside carrying two shopping bags in each hand. Before I was even through the door, Barx practically knocked me over. He had the leash in his mouth, and his tail was wagging wildly.

"You look like you need a walk, huh, boy?"

"Go ahead and take him," Ajji said. "Just drop the bags on the counter and I'll put everything away."

But as soon as I took another step, I tripped and fell onto the floor.

"Oh look at that," Ajji said. "Your kitty is underfoot! He missed you, too. You certainly have a wonderful way with animals, mommaga."

This was too weird. Klawde was never underfoot. What was going on?

While I was picking up the spilled vegetables, Klawde came over and whispered in my ear. "Don't go with Barx! I must talk to you first—it is a matter of vital intergalactic importance!"

"What?" I said.

"I said you have a **wonderful way** with **animals**!" Ajji repeated.

"Right, of course!" I said. Then I turned to Klawde. "Uh, so, *Klawde*," I said loudly, "I have to take Barx for a walk. He needs to pee."

I could see the fury in his eyes. He climbed my

pants leg like I was a tree and mouthed the words:

I HAVE TO TALK TO YOU!

Ajji, shaking her head, came over and pulled him off. "Naughty kitty," she said. "Let them go! Roscoe has to do his business."

Klawde hissed.

"Sorry, Klawde," I said, "but we'll be back soon!"

The rain had turned to a drizzle, so it wasn't too bad a night for a walk. Barx and I passed by Lindy's house and turned down the street that led to the off-leash dog park. Roscoe stopped to sniff at a tree like he was about to pee. But then he bolted away, ripping the leash from my hands.

"Roscoe!" I yelled, sprinting after him. "Come back!"

I chased him for blocks, but he never slowed down and he never looked back. Then suddenly he veered to the right, crashed through a wall of hedges, and disappeared.

I fought my way through the bushes, still calling

his name, until I came out in a vacant lot. A half-built house loomed spookily overhead. It was late and getting harder to see. "Roscoe! Roscoe, *come*!"

He didn't come.

"Roscoe, where are you?"

I was starting to think he was gone forever when I heard a voice.

"I'm right here, Raj."

CHAPTER 34

I leaped from window to window, peering into the darkness, but there was no sign of boy-ogre or spacedog. I did spy Ginger, the orange cat who lived in the fortress behind mine, prowling through the hedges—this despite the awful falling liquid that drenched her fur. (What was *wrong* with these Earth cats?)

Having previously microchipped the ogre, I could tell that he and Barx had not gone far. So why weren't they back yet? What were they doing?

Agitated, I hopped down from the ledge and began to sharpen my claws on the Humans' rug. I should never have let Barx get the boy-ogre alone first! The canine's insistence that I face punishment for my crime was ridiculous—as if a warlord should be held accountable for anything! Nevertheless, I feared an interest in "justice" would take hold in the Human's weak mind.

But he would never allow Barx to take me away.

Would he?

Curses!

I was so flustered that I could not even enjoy tormenting Wuffles. I did it anyway, however. A warrior must never shirk his duty.

CHAPTER 35

"Who's there?" I asked, peering nervously into the dark.

Slowly, from out of the shadows, stepped Roscoe.

"It's me, Raj."

My jaw dropped. "Roscoe, you can *speak*?"

"My name isn't Roscoe," he said. "It is Comrade Barx of ReeTreeVur, the fifty-sixth planet in the Dog Star Cluster. I am a space ranger from the intergalactic peacekeeping force known as PUPPS."

Was this even possible? First an alien cat—and now a **talking spacedog**?

"I think I have to sit down."

"Look, Raj, I'm sure this is a lot for you to take in," he said. "It's probably nearly as shocking as the time Lunabelle Lippman asked you to the fifth-grade dance. Congratulations on *that* by the way."

"You know about Lunabelle?"

"Oh, I know all about your life, Raj!" Barx said, wagging his tail. "I know that you ate Pringles at school today—don't worry, I won't tell Ajji. I know that Sarah, the girl who sits next to you in math, was chewing spearmint gum last week. I know that you went to Disneyland when you were nine. And I know that you peed your pants in front of the entire class when you were a *little* too old to be doing such a thing."

"But—but—how do you know all of this?"

"Well, you know when I sniffed your, um . . ." Barx coughed.

"That's why you kept sticking your nose there?" At first I was totally grossed out, but then I realized: "That's SO COOL! You can smell everything that ever happened to me. It's like you have a superpower!"

Barx bowed his head modestly. "I have been told my nose is particularly keen."

"Why did you come to Earth?" I asked. "Did your spaceship crash-land? Are you stranded here? Are you trying to get back home?"

At this point, Barx turned serious again.

"I have come here on a special mission. And I have some bad news for you, Raj," he said. "Your cat . . . oh, gosh, how do I say this? Your cat . . ."

He was making me really nervous. "My cat *what*?" I said.

"Your cat is an evil warlord."

I let out a big sigh of relief. "Oh, sure, I knew that!"

"Oh, you did? Huh," Barx said, tilting his head to one side. "Well, okay, but that's not all. The thing is, Klawde did something pretty darn awful in my solar system, and the dogs back home aren't just going to let him get away with it. So they sent me here to bring him to justice."

"Wait—you want to take my cat *away*? To be punished?" I said. "You came here to **arrest** him?"

"Well, yes. But I need your permission."

"Why would I ever give you *that*?" I asked. "He's my cat. I love him!"

Barx raised an eyebrow. "Do you know that your cat is trying to leave Earth to go back to Lyttyrboks?" he asked. "The only reason Klawde is still here is because

I surrounded your entire galaxy with an impenetrable electromagnetic force field."

"Okay, first—it is *so cool* you can do that," I said. "And second, I don't care! Klawde is always trying to go back home and conquer his planet. And he always comes back!"

"He still needs to face justice for his crime."

"And just what did he do that was so bad?" I demanded.

The dog now raised both eyebrows and sighed. "I had hoped to spare you the details—I am sure you want to think the best of him. But if you *must* know, your cat . . ." Barx paused, like he wasn't sure how to go on. "Well, he blew up a PLANET."

Klawde? Blowing up an entire planet? I couldn't believe it!

Except, actually, I could.

CHAPTER 36

It was obvious from the moment they came through the front portal that Barx had revealed his true identity to my Human. The boy-ogre wouldn't even look me in the eye. And when I attempted to bestow the Leg Curl upon him, he shook me off.

This was serious.

It was impossible to get him alone until the time the Humans designated to commence their death-like sleep. Once we were in his bedroom, I sprang to the top of the bookshelf as he removed one set of body coverings and replaced them with another. It was an act I would never comprehend.

"I don't know what that miserable mutt told you," I said from atop my perch. "But it was a **lie**! All of it!"

"I *hope* it was a lie." The boy took off his socks and

wadded them into a ball. "He told me that you blew up a planet!"

"Oh, that," I said. "Well, that is true."

"Are you PURRING, Klawde?" the boy-Human demanded. "How could you? You destroyed a whole planet!"

"Well, it wasn't like it was *inhabited*."

"It wasn't?"

"Of course not," I said. "What kind of monster do you think I am?"

"Well, you do talk about skinning your enemies alive a lot."

"That is just pleasant conversation," I said. "Besides, do you have any idea how many planets there are in the universe? What's one less?"

"But it wasn't yours to blow up!"

"Have you learned nothing about what it means to be a warlord? *Everything* is mine."

The young ogre shook his head firmly.

"Well, Barx told me something else," he went on. "He said you're trying to leave Earth, and the only reason you can't go is because he put a force field around the Milky Way. Which is really cool, but I still hope it isn't true."

"Oh *no*, Raj," I said, opening my eyes wide and offering my best look of innocence. "Definitely not. I . . . *HACK* . . . love it here on . . . *HACK! HACK!* . . . Earth. I would never . . . *COUGH* . . . want to leave."

Though I was no expert in Human emotion recognition, I sensed the ogre was not entirely convinced that I was telling the truth.

CHAPTER 37

"So, how's everything at home?" Mom asked when she and Dad called the next day.

I still didn't know what to tell them. Should I mention that the stray dog living in our house was an intergalactic canine bounty hunter? Or that our cat had blown up an entire planet? Or that Ajji was hosting a dinner party for my class that was going to ruin what little social standing I had at school?

"Um, fine. Nothing much is going on."

Mom told me about her parasailing, scuba diving, and language classes, and she was just getting into how she'd won the lei-making contest when:

"Hey, Raj! Raj! Do you have any more of that kibble? I'm starving!"

I turned around to see Barx panting at me.

"Raj, who is that?" my mom asked.

I thought fast. "It's Steve. He's over for a snack."

"And he wants *kibble*?"

"Well, you know Steve. That's his name for—uh—granola! Anyway, gotta go. Love you!"

I hung up the phone.

"The kibble?" Barx asked again. "Please? Now?"

I poured a handful of food into his bowl. The sound woke up Wuffles, who came running to get some, too. Klawde, napping on top of the fridge, didn't even move.

"You almost got caught by my mom," I said to Barx.

"*Thorry!*" he said, his mouth full.

I couldn't get over how much Barx seemed like a regular dog—except for the talking, that is. It was torture for Klawde to adjust to life here, but Barx fit right in. Could it really be so easy for him?

"So isn't it, like, a *little* bit strange to be here on Earth?" I asked.

"Oh not at all!" Barx said. "It's wonderful. (That kibble was so delicious—may I have some more? A little bit more than that? Thanks.) We dogs are used to interplanetary travel. There are so many excellent planets in the Dog Star Cluster. There is PooDill, and TerrEyUr, and HussKee—each one different and special!"

"Have you been to all of them?"

Barx shook his head sadly. "I've been to many. But there was one planet I always hoped to visit. It didn't have much on it, but on clear nights you could see it twinkling brightly, way off in the black sky. Oh, it was beautiful. That is, until SOMEONE blew it up."

Barx looked up at Klawde, who yawned and stretched. "As they say back home," he said, *sticks and stones may break my bones, but a protovoltastic laser will blow up a planet.*"

CHAPTER 38

My calm exterior betrayed nothing to my foe. On the inside, however, I burned with the white-hot fury of a neutron star. Nothing was going as planned. Not only was that wretched spacedog still here, but the force field remained intact, and the ogre now knew everything.

When I called Flooffee to discuss our next steps, he was less than reassuring.

"Well, lord and master, there are still plenty of cats eager for your return. The problem is that the Calico Queen has thrown most of them in prison. I don't think—"

Suddenly the communicator screen filled with static, and Flooffee vanished. A second later, the odious face of my least favorite feline flickered into view.

General Ffangg.

"Why hello there, Klawdie," he purred. "Am I interrupting your secret little conspiracy?"

Hiss!

"It is good to see you too, old friend. And my my my, there is so *much* of you to see." Ffangg smugly groomed his whiskers. "I have a message from your queen."

"That ungrateful kitten is not my queen," I spat. "And you, vile flatterer, are not my friend! You are a two-faced mongrel of the lowest order!"

"Are those the best insults you can muster?" Ffangg asked. "If so, your wits have become as dull as the claws of those idiot dogs with whom you have become so chummy."

"Ha! I am master to those curs, while you cravenly serve a ruler who has yet to lose her kitten whiskers!"

Ffangg offered a hideous smirk. "Such ungratefulness, when here I am, making this call to *help* you. For the message from the Calico Queen is this: If you return to Lyttyrboks, it shall be to meet your doom."

"*Destiny*, you mean!"

"No, I definitely mean *doom*," Ffangg said. He leaned in to the communicator until his face filled the entire screen. "Now, if you will excuse me, I have an army to lead. Don't you have a catnip mouse to play with?" He bared his teeth at me. "Goodbye, Klawde. Or should I say 'mrow'?"

HISS!

CHAPTER 39

As soon as the sun was up, Ajji had me down in the kitchen, scrubbing the counters so we could start preparing for the big feast.

"But it's not until *tomorrow*," I said, blearily stumbling into the kitchen.

"I know!" Ajji said. "And we haven't even begun to prepare the podi!"

These were the spice powder blends. First we had to individually roast each of the spices, and boy were there a lot of them: We were making three kinds of curry powders alone, as well as Ajji's own secret sambar blend, which was my all-time favorite. Once that was done, we had to grind them.

As I crushed the cumin with Ajji's mortar and pestle, I began thinking about everything Barx had said.

And about what he was asking me to do.

Could I give up Klawde? Was he really evil? Like

EVIL evil?

What would life without Klawde even be like? And what would it be like to have a *nice* pet—one who actually showed me affection, like Barx?

But what was I **thinking**?!? I couldn't give away Klawde! No matter how many planets he blew up. And no dog—talking or not—was half the pet Klawde was. He'd rescued me from a crazy camp counselor, built a space teleporter, and trained a battalion of fighting kittens! What had Barx done except a bunch of tricks any dog could do?

And, you know, putting the entire Milky Way on lockdown.

I jammed the pestle down into the mortar. Did not wanting Klawde to be punished for what he'd done make me a terrible person? I *knew* he was an evil alien warlord. I just never knew exactly what that meant.

I looked over at my grandma. She was grating what looked like a dark brown bar of soap.

"What's that?" I asked.

"Oh, you don't know? It is the most important of all spices!" she said. "Here, have a smell."

I took a whiff. *"Ewwww!"* I said. "It's like the world's worst BO! What *is* it?"

"We call it a hing, but in English you call it asafetida." Ajji grinned. "Or devil's dung."

That definitely sounded more accurate.

"Ajji, can I ask you a question?"

"Yes, Raj, you must always grind your own podi."

"No, a different question."

"Oh. Of course."

"What do you do if you find out that one of your friends did something really terrible?"

"Such as tell a lie, you mean?"

"No, not exactly," I said, grinding and thinking. "More like they broke something of someone else's. Like, they destroyed it."

"Well, one must always respect the possessions of others," she said, putting down the devil's dung for a moment. "But possessions are just that—possessions! What is truly important is not doing harm to other living creatures, whether they are people or animals."

I think Ajji could see that that didn't quite answer my question.

"Is this friend a good person?" she asked.

"I'm not sure how to answer that."

"All I can say, Raj, is be loyal to your friends, as you are to your family. No matter how much we may fight or kid, we always stick by one another. That's what you do when you love someone."

She smiled.

"Now, mommaga, put a little more of that muscle of yours into the grinding or we won't be able to have this party until your *next* birthday!"

CHAPTER 40

Painful as it was to admit, there was no getting around it: In order to turn the young ogre to my side, I would have to be *nice* to him.

I was at a disadvantage, I knew. Unlike Barx, I refused to chase balls or pieces of dead trees and bring them back in my mouth. My tail was incapable of the happy, mindless wagging that so delighted Humans. And I would never stoop to "giving kisses."

So I suggested to the ogre that we bond on an intellectual level. Perhaps, I said, we could read some of his "comic books."

"Sure!" he said. He retrieved examples of this most Human form of literature and stretched out on his sleeping platform to peruse them.

I read over his shoulder. "What is this senseless

drivel?" I demanded. "And who drew these crude scribbles? A week-old kitten could do better!" I flipped forward twenty pages, comprehending the entire "plot" in seconds. "Who cares about the trials and tribulations of this supposed alien? Like they even *have* other furless ogres in space! And why is he wearing that cloth around his neck? Is it a giant red napkin?"

"That's Superman's cape," the boy-ogre said. "Look, this was your idea. Maybe you should keep an open mind?"

"An open mind is a weak mind," I said. "A mind should be impenetrable, like a prison!"

"Klawde . . ."

"All right, fine. Yes. It is . . . uh, *fascinating* how the ogres must battle each other wearing . . . such interesting costumes."

Next we tried watching filmed entertainment on a small, crude screen down in the bunker. But if I had thought that ogres would do better with moving pictures, I was wrong. Certainly, I appreciated the outrageous levels of violence and destruction depicted, as well as the advanced powers these super-ogres possessed. (If only *real* Humans were this capable!) The problem was that none of it made **any** sense.

"What does this Iron Ogre have against the handsome alien with the purple face?" I asked.

My Human said something about the one being *good* and the other being *evil*—as if evil were a negative!

We watched several of these entertainments. In each, the supervillain was defeated, despite being smarter, more charming, and infinitely more powerful. This "villain" always got the so-called "hero" into a situation from which there could be no possible escape. And yet somehow this boring and tedious hero would break out of the trap and defeat their omnipotent nemesis, often by demonstrating "loyalty" and "honesty," qualities every warrior knows are useless on the battlefield.

And everywhere else, for that matter.

It was nearly impossible to figure out what in the eighty-seven moons this ogre and I could share feelings over! But perhaps if I *helped* him with something, he would experience maximum affection for me.

So I brought out his homework. "You don't know the square root of 9,801? How many brain cells do you have? Less than 9,801, clearly! The answer is 99, you furless dolt!!!"

The boy-ogre frowned at me, but he wrote the answer down.

"Excellent! Now that we have 'bonded,' you must send that wretched mutt HOME."

"I definitely appreciate how you're trying to be nice, Klawde," he said. "But the answer is no."

CHAPTER 41

It was weird enough having two talking pets, but it was even weirder now that they were fighting over me.

"Hey, Raj, look!" Klawde said, walking into my room. "Your plastic fang-cleaner! I have 'fetched' it for you so you will have the emotion of 'love' for me."

He was holding my toothbrush in his mouth. By the bristles.

"That's gross, Klawde," I said, taking it away from him. "And why do you keep using my name? You never do that."

"I am trying new things here on your wonderful planet," he said, *"which I have absolutely no plans to ever leave."*

I was glad that Klawde wanted to spend more time with me lately. Could it be that he was worried that I liked Barx better than him?

Probably not. More likely, he was afraid I'd let Barx take him to the Dog Star Cluster to face punishment.

But if I didn't let Barx take him, would Klawde leave on his own? He said that he wouldn't. But he also said things like "Lies are the sharpest arrows in the warrior's quiver" and "The truth is whatever I say it is."

I headed downstairs. Barx was lying at the foot of the staircase and immediately popped up when he heard me. "Raj! Raj! Do you want to go play, Raj?"

"Um . . ." The truth was, I was kind of tired. Also my arm was sore from throwing his ball every day for hours. "How about in a little while? Ajji wants me to clean for the party tomorrow."

Barx sat down. "Okay! No problem! I can wait." He looked out the window for a moment. Then he turned back to me and stood up, tail wagging. "Are you ready **now**?"

"That was like five seconds, Barx," I said.

"Sorry, Raj! Sorry! I just get so excited." He sat back down, but his tail still wagged.

I'd never realized how much work it was to have a dog, let alone a talking one.

"Is that enough time?" Barx asked. "Can we play now? No? How about *now*? Oh shoot, am I annoying you? I'll stop annoying you. Wait, I'm still doing it, aren't I? *Bad dog!*"

I rolled my eyes. "You're not a bad dog," I said.

"Yes he is," Klawde said, walking past us in the hallway.

Barx panted at me. "Now?" he said. "Now, Raj? Ball?"

CHAPTER 42

How dreadful it was to be kind. And confusing! How could the ogre not like it when I groomed his horrifyingly smooth face? Did he think **I** enjoyed it?

"Kindness is like a game of fetch!" Barx said. "You throw a great big ball of love out into the world as hard as you can, and it comes racing right back to you!"

I sharpened my claws on the dining room chair. "That's the stupidest thing I have ever heard. Also, isn't 'fetch' what made the ogre your master, and you his *pet*?" I spat out the word with all the scorn I could muster.

"Call it whatever you want. The relationship Raj and I share doesn't need labels," Barx said. "Hey, you're scratching the wood. You should stop that."

"The 'relationship' you share is a disgrace to all advanced four-legged beings! You should be humiliated."

"As if!" Barx said. "I haven't felt so happy since I was a pup burying my first bone." He squinted off into the distance. "I never did find that bone . . ."

Thankfully, my communicator rang, saving me from any further inane discussion. But I knew the moment I saw my lackey's face that something was amiss.

"Supreme Leader, the loyalists are about to give up and swear an oath of loyalty to the Calico Queen!" Flooffee said. "If you don't get that dog to take down the force field soon, the rescue ship won't ever come!"

Hiss!!

I turned to my nemesis. "The ogre must make his decision. Now."

"*At leashed* let me have one last game of fetch with him!" Barx said. "*At leashed*—get it? Because Raj takes me out on a *leash*?"

If only I could beat him over the head with that wagging tail of his.

CHAPTER 43

The day I'd been dreading—the day of my party—had finally arrived. The house was clean, the dining room table was set, and the balloons Ajji had insisted on buying were bobbing around the ceiling. But even though we'd started preparations days ago, the food still wasn't quite finished.

While Ajji was putting up streamers in the living room, I was rolling out roti and cooking them. Or trying to. I was just about to burn another one when Klawde and Barx came into the kitchen.

"Can we have a *word*?" Klawde asked.

"Hold on," I said, plucking a roti from the tava. "*Hot! Hot!* I'm kinda busy here."

"Oh sure!" Barx said. "You look like you're working hard, Raj! Do you want some help? Do you need any bowls licked? Any food I should try? Maybe you want me to welcome the guests?"

"Human, NOW!" Klawde said.

Since I wasn't doing a very good job with the roti anyway, I turned off the stove. "All right, let's go into the garage."

"Who is that talking, Raj?" Ajji called. "Did some of your friends get here early?"

"No, it was me—I was just talking to the animals!" I called back. "I have to go out to the car. I, uh, left something in the back seat."

The moment we got into the garage, Wuffles started barking. I forgot that he'd taken to hiding in there to avoid Klawde.

"It's okay, little buddy," Barx said. "There's nothing to be afraid of."

"That's what you think," Klawde muttered. Then he turned to me. "Now listen up, ogre—I mean *Raj*. I am putting my paw down. The time has come for you to send this insufferable do-gooder home!"

"That would be fine," Barx said, "so long as you send this cat criminal *with* me."

I looked back and forth between Klawde and Barx. What was I supposed to do?

"Raj," Barx said, a look of sympathy filling his big brown eyes. "You are conflicted, I understand. All too well, because I am also conflicted. Do you think I *want* to leave this paradise called Earth? But each of us must do our duty as a cosmic citizen and try to bend this vast and crazy universe of ours toward justice! All it takes is just one small act of bravery—a decision to side with what is *right* and *decent* and *good* instead of with . . . Klawde." Barx stood tall, and his luxurious golden coat gleamed. "Send this misguided feline off to face his most well-deserved punishment."

You couldn't deny it, the dog was pretty convincing.

"Klawde," I said, looking over to my cat. "What do you have to say?"

"What do *I* have to say?" Klawde spat. "I have to say that was utter drivel! If that ludicrous nonsense is the *best* this mutt can do, then he's made my case for me. The defense rests!"

I sighed. Klawde wasn't making my decision easier. But it didn't matter.

"Look, Barx, you're an amazing dog, and I'm sure a really great space ranger. The universe is a better place for having you in it. As for you, Klawde . . ." I paused. "Well, I'm not sure what to say, other than that you're more than my cat. You're a member of my family, and I can't send you away."

Klawde curled his tail around his paws and began to purr.

CHAPTER 44

At last! My exhausting kindness to the boy-ogre had paid off, and victory was mine.

Barx had a pathetic hangdog look about him. It was delicious. Unfortunately, I had no chance to savor it.

"I didn't want to have to do this," the miserable cur said, "but I've been left with no choice."

The dog then unleashed the greatest tactical weapon in his arsenal—his face! The eyes of Barx widened. His ears lifted, and his head cocked far to one side.

It was the most pleading look I had ever seen.

"It's some sort of hypnosis!" I shouted. "A canine mind trick! Resist, ogre! **RESIST!!!!**"

My words fell on deaf ears. The ogre was falling into a trance, mesmerized by the dog's hypnotic gaze!

But then—thank the eighty-seven moons!—the intruder alert rang.

DING-DONG!

"Raj!" the ancient ogre called from the kitchen. "It's your first guest! Where *are* you?"

The ogre jumped as if pinched, shook his head in confusion, and then headed out of the garage.

"*STAY!*" he commanded, pausing in the doorway. "And that means you, too, Klawde!"

CHAPTER 45

I was relieved to see that Cedar and Steve were the first to arrive. Too bad Newt and Scorpion were right behind them.

I couldn't believe it. They were *crashing* my birthday party!

"Hello, children," Ajji said, beaming at them. "I am so glad you could come!" She held out a plate of pakoras and samosas. "Please, help yourself."

Scorpion made a face but took one, and so did Newt.

Pretty soon more people showed up, including Max, Brody, and Sarah from math. Lindy came in with Chad, who had a big bow attached to his harness. Ajji told everyone to leave their presents on the coffee table and then come into the dining room.

"I hope you brought your appetites!" she said.

She'd finished making the roti, and the food lay steaming on the table: great big bowls of rice, dal, sambar, and all kinds of curries and side dishes.

I held my breath. What would everyone say?

Steve leaned over the buffet table like he was about to dive into a pool. "This looks *awesome*," he said.

Steve, of course, would eat anything. It was the other kids I was worried about. I was too nervous to talk to any of them, so I just helped myself to a bowl of sambar. They all started to fill up their plates, but none of them looked too excited about it.

When I noticed that Ajji had garnished the pakora platter with the crazy-spicy little green chilis that I loved, I picked one up and nibbled on the end. Then I noticed Scorpion about to pop an entire one into his mouth.

"I don't think you want to do that," I said. "Those peppers are deadly."

"This little thing?" Scorpion sneered. "If you can eat

it, *I* can eat it. I once drank a whole glass of sriracha!"

"Okay, but don't say I didn't warn you."

Scorpion popped the pepper into his mouth and bit it off at the stem. Instantly, his face turned pink. Then red. And then something close to purple. He ran into the kitchen, stuck his mouth under the faucet, and began guzzling water, drenching his whole head in the process.

Ajji hurried over and patted him on the back. "There, there, you must have raita to cool the burn. Yogurt works much better than water. And have some roti!"

I went upstairs to get him a towel. By the time I got back, Scorpion was happily munching on roti and raita, and everyone else had found something they liked, too. Newt, who had completely filled her plate, lifted up a forkful of bisi bele bath—spicy lentils and rice—and stared at it.

"Do you think it's weird?" I asked her.

"Weird?" she said. "My grandma serves rice gruel with oysters and fermented fish sauce. For breakfast. This . . ." She took a giant bite. "This is regular."

Brody laughed. "*My* grandma makes baked turnips and tofu. It's so gross!"

"My grandma just microwaves frozen chicken casseroles," Steve said.

Ajji grinned at me like *I told you this would work.*

I couldn't believe it. Everyone was smiling and laughing. And eating!

But I barely had any time to enjoy it, because suddenly I heard hissing and growling coming from the direction of the garage.

"What ifff that fffound?" Steve said with his mouth full of pakora.

"It sounds like a Tasmanian devil fighting a rabid dingo," Cedar said.

"You guys stay here," I said. "I'll take care of it."

And I broke into a run.

CHAPTER 46

"Your little canine mind trick didn't work!" I gloated. "So much for *man's best friend*. Now you heard the ogre: **Go home!**"

Barx didn't budge. "Actually," he said, "Raj never gave me that command. So, here we are. *Still*." He sat down and glared at me.

My whiskers trembled in rage. I jumped to the hood of the Humans' go-cart, from which I could stare down into Barx's mud-brown eyes. Our noses practically touched.

"You and your absurd canine technicalities!" I thundered. "Just leave! *Go home!* Don't you get it? I will never face justice. *You failed*. You are a bad dog. A **bad dog**!"

A low growl started in Barx's throat, and the fur

along his spine began to rise up.

"Don't you growl at me!" I said, slashing him across his hideous snout.

Barx bared every single one of his deadly teeth.

"RRRRRARRRRRR!"

I believe this is what the ancients were referring to when they said: *There comes a moment in every warrior's life when he must retract his claws and RUN.*

CHAPTER 47

I'd only made it halfway across the kitchen when the door to the garage banged open. I saw a blur of blue-gray zoom by me—Klawde—followed by a golden streak—Barx. Wuffles (definitely not a blur) brought up the rear, barking his head off.

"Stop it, you guys!" I shouted.

I should have known that wouldn't work.

Klawde raced into the dining room, jumped onto the buffet table, and then sprinted up and down the length of it, leaping over bowls of curry. Barx ran around the table in circles, his big jaws snapping at Klawde's back paws. Then Barx banged into Brody, who lost his balance and fell, taking his plate of food down with him. As he went, his elbow shot up and sent Max's plate flying into Newt's face. Scorpion started to laugh, but then Klawde's back feet kicked *his* plate—right onto his pants. Scorpion's face got all red again.

I was still yelling, **"Stop! Stop!"** and still none of them were listening.

Then Barx grabbed the corner of the tablecloth and started tugging, pulling Klawde—*and* all the platters of food—toward him.

Everyone tried to grab the bowls before they went over the edge, but there were too many of them! Thinking quickly, Cedar tossed a huge roti at Barx, who let go of the tablecloth and caught it like a Frisbee.

But that wasn't the end of the chaos. Klawde sprang down to the floor, and then all the animals were racing around the room again. Lindy swooped up Chad, but he scrambled out of her arms and leaped to a window ledge.

Wait—was that my *Oklo* attached to his harness?

Before I could get a closer look, Klawde shot through my legs. I tried to grab his tail but missed.

Then I went to tackle Barx, but he dodged me and barreled into Sarah, who fell back against the wall.

Ajji stuck her fingers in her mouth and let loose a crazy-loud whistle. Then she yelled, **"Who wants a treat?"**

Klawde and Barx stopped in their tracks and looked up at her. She was holding up two big cubes of cheese.

"Paneer!" they both said at once.

As the suddenly calm animals began to eat, Cedar said, "That was a really strange meow. Even for Klawde."

"And it almost sounded like the dog . . . was *talking*!" Scorpion said.

"I think that pepper's gone to your head," I said.

Steve looked particularly concerned about what was going on.

"Hey," he said. "Can *I* get some of that paneer?"

CHAPTER 48

It had been far too long since I had witnessed such satisfying mayhem.

The room looked like the scene of a deadly battle. Instead of blood pooling upon the ground, however, there was curry. The Humans encouraged the canines and me to devour it, as they superstitiously believe that food becomes spoiled the instant it touches the ground.

Next came the strangest Human behavior I had yet witnessed. The ancient one brought out a cake with the name and age of my ogre upon it. She then set it *on fire*. Just as I began to fear for his life, the other ogres gathered around him to chant an earsplitting ode to his birth. At the end of this song, my Human extinguished the flames by blowing air on them. In an apparent reward for this accomplishment, he was presented with useless objects wrapped in colorful paper.

This arcane ritual completed, the other young ogres left, with the exception of the one belonging to Flabby. I could wait no longer, however. It was time to settle the dog problem once and for all.

I called Floofee and commanded him to depart Lyttyrboks in the escape pod immediately.

"So Barx let down the force field?" he asked.

"Not yet! But he will!"

After summoning my ogre and my enemy back to the garage, I calmly requested that the former send the latter home in shame. "NOW! Or you will feel the pain of my wrath!"

When the boy-ogre did not respond, I tried a different tactic. I widened my eyes. I cocked my head. I tried to look pleading. And . . . *cute*.

"Is something wrong with your face, Klawde? Quit that, it looks weird," he said. "Anyway, I'm not going to send Barx away if he doesn't want to go. Just like I wasn't going to send you off to some dog prison."

"Who said anything about *prison*?" Barx said, a look of horror upon his face. "We canines outlawed kennels thousands of years ago."

"Wait—so if you're not sending Klawde to prison," my ogre asked, "then what **is** his punishment?"

"The only thing that makes any sense," Barx said stiffly.

By this, I assumed he meant clipping my whiskers and stringing me up by my claws, as any reasonable being would.

"Klawde has to make amends," Barx continued in a grave manner. "He must . . . *say he's sorry.*"

"**What?**" I said.

"That's *it*?" my ogre yelped.

"Well, he never *has* said it," Barx said indignantly. "And one should apologize after blowing up a planet."

The boy-ogre wagged a finger at me. "Yes, one definitely should," he said.

I took a deep breath in.

"If that is what it must be," I said in my grimmest voice, "I will bear the awful indignity."

Oh, how hard it was to stifle my purr of glee! Awful indignity? Ha! I could hardly believe my luck! What goody-goody morons these dogs were. Apologize? Nothing was easier! As even the dullest kitten knows: *Good things come to those who lie.*

"All righty then," Barx said. "I guess we can take off for the Dog Star Cluster!"

"But wait," the boy-ogre said. "Why does Klawde have to go across the universe? Can't he apologize to you right here? Right now?"

It was a shrewd observation by my ogre. How unexpected.

Due to the Master Clause, Barx had no choice

but to do as the Human requested. Using his collar, he summoned the image of the canine called Muffee and explained the situation. She promptly called for an emergency meeting of their security council, and one by one an entire pack of spacedogs appeared.

Oh, this was going to be *fun*.

CHAPTER 49

Wow! Doggie holograms! It was like some sci-fi movie, except it was real, and it was happening *inside my garage*.

There were a million questions I wanted to ask the dog aliens, but they weren't paying any attention to me. They listened silently while the little brown-and-white pooch read an account of Klawde's crime. It looked to me like Klawde was loving every minute of it, but none of them seemed to notice.

I didn't think there was any way he'd apologize. But I was wrong.

Sort of.

"Comrade Muffee. Esteemed representatives of the Dog Star Cluster," Klawde said when it was his turn to speak. "Before you stands that rarest of creatures: a remorseful feline. Regret fills me, from the end of my tail to the tips of my whiskers. If I could turn back time and not blow Rumpz to smithereens, I would do so. It was a majestic little speck of a planet, and it did not deserve its fate. Only in my careless youth could I have committed such a reckless act."

He was laying it on pretty thick.

"I never thought he'd be this apologetic!" Barx whispered to me. "He's so *sincere!*"

It was funny how Barx could sniff out my fifth-grade crush on Lunabelle Lippman, but not Klawde's totally obvious sarcasm. The hologram dogs seemed to be buying it, too.

"The pleasure of watching Rumpz explode into trillions of subatomic particles is nothing compared to the sorrow I feel now, knowing that I have caused pain to you, you innocent, friendly, aromatic dogs," Klawde said.

At that moment, a blinking red light caught my

eye, and I saw Chad creeping closer to Klawde. That was *definitely* my Okto on his harness.

And it was recording!

"I hope that someday you will find it in your great and generous doggie hearts to forgive me, lowly feline that I am," Klawde said. And then he did something I could *not* believe.

Klawde rolled over on his back, and he showed them his belly.

"Well, that's good enough for me," Barx said. "Comrade Muffee?"

Muffee nodded. "I declare that this feline is truly sorry and has served his punishment," she announced. "But, as always, the verdict of the Pack must be unanimous. What say my fellow Alpha Dogs?"

"*WOOWOOWOOWOOWOO!*" the dogs all went.

Except one.

"Comrade Fydo," Muffee said, "you are not satisfied?"

The old bulldog grunted. "I miss howling at Rumpz as it rose at night," she said.

"There's no bringing the planet back," Barx said. "And clearly, Klawde *is* sorry. Just look at him!"

Klawde had that totally fake pleading look on his face again.

"Oh *fine*," Fydo said, rolling her eyes. "Woo woo woo."

"Wyss-Kuzz of Lyttyrboks," Comrade Muffee said, "I now declare your punishment . . . *served*!"

With that, the hologram flickered, and the spacedogs disappeared.

And that's when I heard Ajji yelling for me.

"Raj, I know you love your animals," she called, "but I need some help with this mess!!"

"Raj! Hey, Raj!" Barx said. "I'll help you *retrieve* dishes from the dining room! Because I'm a golden *retriever*, get it?"

"Uh, yeah," I said, rolling my eyes. "Ha. Good one."

CHAPTER 50

I blocked the cur from following the boy-Human.

"I fulfilled my end of the bargain," I said. "Now you must fulfill yours!"

He cocked his giant yellow head in confusion. "Oh, right!" he said, finally getting it. "The force field!"

Barx opened the app on his collar and entered the password:

:)PEACE_LOVE_AND_HAPPINESS:)

Such gibberish! No wonder I couldn't crack it.

The moment the idiot canine left, I, too, exited the garage and made my way into the yard to await Flooffee's arrival. I waited and waited, and waited still more.

Blast it! Where *was* he? Entire Earth minutes had passed!

I was about to call my minion to berate him when I

caught sight of the ship. The rescue module descended, the portal opened, and Flooffee poked his head out. "Greetings, O All-Conquering Lord!"

"Where have you **been**?" I demanded.

"Sorry!" Flooffee said. "Exploding supernova in the Quartian Quadrant. And—oh wow! Is that who I think it is?"

From behind me came a voice. *"Mrowr?"*

"Flabby!" Flooffee cried, jumping down from the module just as I was leaping atop it.

"What are you doing, fool?" I said. "We have to **go**!"

Ignoring me, the imbecile trotted over to Flabby, the even greater imbecile. "It's my old Earth pal!" Flooffee cried. "How've you been, buddy? Looks like you've kept your appetite up!"

"Mrowr! Mrowr!"

"Yeah, you don't have to tell *me* he can be tough to work for," Flooffee muttered. "And look! You still have

the camera on! And you've been recording. The cats back home have been *dying* for more of your videos!"

"LEAVE IT!" I commanded.

"Are you sure—"

"Now!" I cried. "There is only one thing we must do: **return to Lyttyrboks**!"

Flooffee hung his head and slunk back into the ship, and I took one last look at the place that had been my home lo these many months.

Peace out, ogres!

Glory would soon be mine.

CHAPTER 51

Ajji and Lindy were at the sink washing dishes when I came into the kitchen.

"Great news!" Lindy said as I grabbed a broom. "Your grandma told me I can adopt Wuffles!"

Ajji smiled. "What I actually said was that after we finish cleaning up, we can go talk to her parents." She turned to Lindy. "And if they say it's okay, we can fill out the Furever Doggie adoption application."

"That's awesome," I said. I meant it, too. I just hoped Lindy's parents had a high tolerance for dog farts.

As I swept, Barx trotted into the kitchen and started helping me clean the floor—with his tongue. When the dishes were done, Ajji went to take Lindy across the street.

"There's leftover paneer in the fridge for the animals if they're hungry," she said as she put on her shoes.

"Oh, Chad might like that, too. But where is he?" Lindy said. She looked around and then shrugged. "Oh, he must be playing with your kitty. I'll come get him later."

As the front door slammed shut, Barx said, "About that paneer . . ."

I had just pulled a bowl of it out of the fridge when I noticed colored lights flashing along the kitchen wall. Was there a cop car outside? An ambulance? I went over to the window and looked out.

No . . . freaking . . . way.

There was a small, egg-shaped spaceship hovering right above my backyard! It was covered in thousands of tiny, blinking lights, and it spun slowly, around and around. It was the most incredible thing I'd ever seen!

"Barx," I gasped, "is that yours?"

"That heap of junk?" he said. "Nope, that looks like it's—"

"**Klawde!**" I hollered.

I ran for the back door, but the lock was sticky and it took me forever to get it open. By the time I burst into the yard, calling for my cat, the hatch to the spaceship had closed and the whole thing was spinning faster. It floated a little higher, and then, suddenly, it was *gone*!

I looked all around. I saw a tail peeking out from behind the elm tree.

"Klawde? Is that you?"

"*Mrowr!*" It was Chad. He waddled over to me. "*Mrowr?*"

He was the only cat in the yard.

I sank down onto the damp grass. I couldn't believe it. Klawde was actually *gone*.

Barx came and sat beside me. "Wow, Raj," he sighed, "that's a real bummer." He paused, panting. "Maybe we should play that game of fetch we were talking about. You know, to take your mind off things?"

I didn't answer. Klawde had gone back to Lyttyrboks. And he'd done it—*could it be true?*—without even saying goodbye.

"You let down the force field," I said.

Barx slowly nodded. "I did. And now I feel like I let *you* down, too."

"It's not your fault," I said.

After a minute, Barx gently put his paw on my leg. "Would rubbing my tummy make you feel better?"

He lay down, and I put my hand in the soft golden fur of his belly. And it *did* make me feel a tiny bit better.

"Oh, yeah, that's the spot," Barx said. "Look, my leg is twitching! See that? I'm not even doing it on purpose!"

I stopped.

"I can't believe he just *left* like that," I said.

"Maybe he'll come back! You said he always does," Barx said. "And maybe I will, too."

"Wait—what?" I said. "You have to leave now, *too*?"

"My mission is over, and I have to go home. The job of being a peacekeeping space ranger dog never ends," Barx said solemnly. "But Earth looks like a lovely place to retire! Maybe I'll come back to live out my *golden* years. Get it? Because I'm a *golden* retriever." Barx wagged his tail.

Klawde was right about one thing. Barx really did have a terrible sense of humor.

CHAPTER 52

What fanfare would greet me in the streets of Lyttyrboks! Parades, military drills, feasting, speeches, and the ritual humiliation of the deposed calico. Perhaps I myself would be the one to shave her tail!

Purr.

"The crowds have amassed at the Imperial Palace," Flooffee said, scanning the ship's monitor. "If all is going according to schedule, the loyalists should be preparing the Scepter of Power for its transfer to you, O Great and Omnipotent Leader."

My whiskers stiffened with pride. "I hereby establish a new and magnificent intergalactic holiday," I declared. "The Triumphal Day of Homecoming and Vengeance! To celebrate the day when I—Wyss-Kuzz, Master of Three Species—returned to Lyttyrboks. Soon I will be back where I belong, seated upon the Most High Throne, ruling my subjects with an iron paw!"

As we entered the atmosphere of Lyttyrboks and floated down to its surface, I spied the swirling masses gathered outside the Imperial Palace. There were cats of every shape, size, and color—all coming together to bow down before me!

Even from that height, I could hear the chanting of the crowd. They were calling for blood! A battle was imminent! Any moment now they would be ready to tear that treacherous calico limb from spotted limb!

Flooffee's communicator rang.

"Uh-huh . . . Uh-huh . . . Wait, *what*?" he said as the ship entered landing mode. "Are you **sure**? . . . The video . . . It was of *what*? . . . You're *positive*? . . . Uh-huh . . . Okay . . . Uh, yeah, goodbye."

My minion looked like he had eaten his own tail.

"What is it, fool?" I yelled. "Is there some delay in

the re-coronation ceremony? Did they fail to get the gallows erected in time? Are there not enough flowers to lay at my paws as I proceed to the throne?"

"Uh, *well*," Flooffee said as the ship touched ground, "do you see that angry mob rushing toward us?"

"Yes!" I said. "It warms my bloodthirsty heart!"

"Well, um, it's not the calico's head they want. It's, uh . . ." Flooffee paused. "*Yours*."

"What?" I thundered. "Why?"

Just then, the escape pod started to rock. We were being swarmed by the infuriated mob!

"Well, er, it might be because of that last video."

My eyes narrowed to slits. "*What* last video?"

"Um, well, when I saw Flabby there in the yard, I noticed he still had the camera on, and you know how popular your films have been . . ."

"Flabby filmed a video *today*?" I demanded. "And you . . . *sent* it?"

"I didn't know it showed you rolling over and begging dogs for forgiveness!" he said. "Did you really mean that?"

"Of course not, you **IMBECILE**!" I roared.

There would be time enough to skin my worthless lackey alive later. Right now, Flooffee had to pilot us out of there. The mob was clawing at the hatch, trying to pry it open.

"What are you *waiting* for?" I screamed. "Engage the lift thrusters!"

"I did! But there are too many cats on top of the ship!" Flooffee said. "The thrusters don't have enough power!"

I searched my memory for what brilliant piece of advice the ancients had for just such a situation.

Unfortunately, there wasn't any.

CHAPTER 53

I was throwing the ball one last time for Barx when my phone rang.

I dug it out of my pocket. The screen read:

SUPREMEST ALL-POWERFUL WARLORD

The ball fell from my hands as I scrambled to answer it.

"Klawde? Is that really you?" I said. "Are you calling me from *outer space*?"

"Indeed it is I, ogre! I am calling you from beside the highest spire atop the Imperial Palace."

The connection was terrible, but I could hear him. My cat! From across the universe!

"Is that where they crown you Ultimate Eternal Warlord or whatever?" I asked.

"Unfortunately, *no*," Klawde shouted above the roar of what sounded like a million cats. "It is where they impale those whom the mob has turned against."

"What do you mean?"

He quickly told me how Flabby Tabby—I mean Chad—had filmed his apology to the dogs, and how it had been broadcast all across Lyttyrboks.

"Wait—with *my Okto*?" I asked. "How did he learn how to use it? And how did the video get sent across the universe? I knew you were up to something when I couldn't find that thing!"

"Ogre, there is no time for irrelevant explanations!"

While Klawde and I were talking, Barx had disappeared into a bush in the corner of the yard. Now he was backing out of it, tugging hard on something in his jaws. A moment later, a small spaceship emerged from the leaves.

There had been a UFO in my yard this whole time!

"Listen to me, ogre," Klawde said. "I have mere moments left to live."

"Klawde—you're not serious," I said, suddenly panicked. "You're exaggerating, right? Like the way you talk about boiling the blood of your enemies?"

"Do not mourn for me! A warrior is courageous, even when facing certain death," Klawde said.

"Klawde, we can *do* some—"

"Be **quiet**, ogre! I am making my final speech!" Klawde yelled. "There is only one thing I have ever felt truly sorry for. And it is that I did not say goodbye to you. And so now: *goodbye*. You were a good 'friend,' Raj Banerjee of Earth."

"Klawde!" I cried. But the phone had gone dead.

I turned to Barx, who had climbed into his spaceship. His tongue hung out eagerly.

I looked him straight in the eye. We both knew what we had to do.

"Barx," I commanded. *"FETCH!"*

CHAPTER 54

I could not believe how poorly my return to Lyttyrboks had gone. After being dragged from my spaceship, hauled to the top of the Imperial Palace, and forced to bow down before my two nemeses, I had used the customary last phone call to contact the boy-ogre. (A curious choice, I know.)

That done, only one task remained for me in this life: to face execution more bravely than any feline ever had! I turned in the direction of my two tormentors and spat.

"*Mrow, mrow, mrow!*" said the calico tyrant. "*MROW!*"

Ffangg arched his back and sighed. "What I believe the queen is trying to say is: *You, Wyss-Kuzz the Terrible, Friend to Ogres and Apologist to Dogs, are about to take your final nap. Do you have any last words?*"

I stood on the very tips of my claws. My tail was as proud as a flag. "It is with GREAT JOY that I will meet the ancient masters of Mew-Jytzu on the other side of the eighty-seven moons!" I roared to the mob. "May the name Wyss-Kuzz forever be an inspiration to every defenseless kitten who dares to dream of one day becoming a cruel and merciless tyrant!"

But then, at the very apex of my oration, with the crowd transfixed, a red flash lit the sky, and I found myself being sucked upward by a powerful tractor beam!

My enemies stared up at me in shock. A small spacecraft hovering high above the palace was *rescuing* me.

Ha! I knew it could never end this way! Of course the loyalists would save me. They were more loyal than anyone could have imagined! Oh righteous joy! Together we would make the calico pay for her treachery. And Ffangg! And the entire worthless mob!

"I will be back!" I howled down to my enemies, growing smaller and smaller below me. "Bringing with me the power and rage of a thousand supernovas!"

With that, I was sucked into the sleek rescue craft, and the hatch closed beneath me. I looked about the interior of the ship. The sophistication and technology were unparalleled! If the loyalists had more ships like this, we would be invincible! The pilot—my rescuer—was seated in the captain's chair, and had not yet faced me.

"Your timing is impeccable, fellow warrior!" I said. "Turn around so that I can thank you properly."

"Don't mention it, chief! I'm glad to help!"

The chair rotated toward me, and my jaw fell open.

It was Barx.

NOOOOO!

CHAPTER 55

"The abomination! The infamy! The appalling indignity of . . . of . . . HACK HACK!" Klawde coughed up the most massive hairball I'd ever seen, right into my mom's potted parsley plant. "Of being rescued by a **DOG**!"

The three of us were in the backyard, and Barx's spaceship was once again parked under our rose bush. Klawde, who'd started ranting the moment the hatch opened, had hardly stopped for a breath since.

"I will never live this down, not in nine thousand lives!"

Even for Klawde, this seemed like a bit of an overreaction. "Geez," I said, "would you have rather *died*?"

Klawde looked at me like I was insane.

"Of course I would have!" he said. "I would rather be impaled a hundred times and die an honorable death than get saved by a slobbering canine!" He pinned his ears back. "Especially *this* slobbering canine."

"Well, Klawde," Barx said, "you're welcome anyway. And now it is time for *me* to go. But don't worry, guys—*somehowl* we'll meet again. Get it, *somehowl*?"

I knew this moment had to come, but I got a lump in my throat just the same. "I'll really miss you, Barx," I said. I reached out and patted his soft yellow head. "You were a really, really good boy."

Barx held up his paw for me to shake. "So were you."

CHAPTER 56

There were not enough hairballs in the universe to express my feelings of revulsion at this grotesque display of sentimentality. The eyes of the Human began to leak, and he said in a choking voice, "I'll never forget you, Do-Good Space Ranger Dog!"

"Nor I you, Beautiful Human Ball-Throwing Boy," Barx sniffed.

As we watched his ship depart in a red flash—so much less attractive than the feline green—I could think of at least one good thing about Earth: It had one less canine on it.

"Don't worry, Klawde," the Human said, wiping his eyes. "We'll be okay. Even though you'll never say it, I know how much you'll miss Barx."

Hiss!

"Ow!" the boy-ogre yelped. "Hey, Klawde, that's real blood there!"

A second good thing about Earth: easily wounded Humans.

CHAPTER 57

When my parents got home a few days later, life returned to normal—except for the fact that everyone at school kept asking me when my grandma was going to throw another awesome party. That felt sort of weird. Nice, but still weird.

My mom was tanned and relaxed, and suddenly she could speak Japanese. My dad, on the other hand, was exactly the same, except for being actually paler than usual.

"Wow, Raj," he said, flopping down into his recliner, "those periodontists are total party animals! I need a few days of vacation just to recover!"

My mom rolled her eyes. "They hung out all day at the pool. Not *in* the pool, mind you, but around it, on deck chairs. And did I mention this was the *indoor* pool?"

Dad handed me a sloppily wrapped present. "This is for you, Raj."

I opened it and unfolded a T-shirt. It had a really bad drawing of Luke Skywalker holding a dental drill. MAY THE FLOSS BE WITH YOU, it read.

"I got you one because you always say how much you like *my* cool dentist T-shirts!"

Apparently Earth fathers weren't much better than spacedogs when it came to picking up on sarcasm.

"Thanks, Dad," I said. "It's *super* cool."

Ajji put an arm around my mom's shoulders. "We had a lovely time while you were gone," she said. "Though I wish you could have met that nice dog, Roscoe."

I'd told Ajji that his owners had finally seen the posters we put up and had come to get him, and she believed me. Why wouldn't she?

Mom looked around. "Wait. Speaking of dogs, where's Wuffles? Shouldn't he be barking his head off at Klawde?"

Ajji grinned. "Oh, that's the best part. Wuffles has found his forever home—right across the street!"

"Well, that seems like a happy ending," Mom said.

Ajji gave me a big hug. "Raj, my dear mommaga, I loved spending time with you. I hope you have learned your lesson about using fresh spices. Perhaps you can teach your mother, too."

"I heard that, Amma," Mom said. Then she laughed.

I nodded. "Thanks for everything, Ajji."

She bent down to Klawde. "I left some paneer for you, naughty kitty. Don't you forget your ajji, now!"

Klawde did that twirl thing around her shins, which was as sweet a thing as I had ever seen him do.

Then he went and threw up.

In Dad's shoe.

"Seriously, Klawde?" my dad shouted.

"He's just glad you're home," I said.

And Klawde gave a mighty hiss.

ABOUT THE AUTHORS

Although a worthless Human, **Johnny Marciano** has redeemed himself somewhat by chronicling the glorious adventures of Klawde, Evil Alien Warlord Cat. His lesser work concerns the pointless doings of other worthless Humans, in books such as *The Witches of Benevento*, *The No-Good Nine*, and *Madeline at the White House*. He currently resides on the planet New Jersey.

Emily Chenoweth is a despicable Human living in Portland, Oregon, where the foul liquid known as rain falls approximately 140 days a year. Under the top secret alias Emily Raymond, she has collaborated with James Patterson on numerous best-selling books. There are three other useless Humans in her family, and two extremely ignorant Earth cats.